Also by Daniel Pinkwater
Published by Farrar, Straus and Giroux

5 Novels

(Alan Mendelsohn, the Boy from Mars;
Slaves of Spiegel; The Snarkout Boys and the Avocado
of Death; The Last Guru; Young Adult Novel)

THE EDUCATION OF
ROBERT NIFKIN

THE EDUCATION OF
ROBERT NIFKIN

DANIEL PINKWATER

Farrar, Straus & Giroux • New York

Copyright © 1998 by Daniel Pinkwater
Title-page art copyright © 1998 by Jill Pinkwater
All rights reserved
Distributed in Canada by Douglas & McIntyre Ltd.
Printed in the United States of America
Designed by Judith M. Lanfredi
First edition, 1998
Second printing, 1998

Library of Congress Cataloging-in-Publication Data
Pinkwater, Daniel Manus. 1941-
    The education of Robert Nifkin / Daniel Pinkwater. — 1st ed.
        p.   cm.
    Summary: Set in the 1950s in Chicago, Robert Nifkin tells his highly unorthodox
high school experiences in the form of a college application essay.
    ISBN 0-374-31969-3
    [1. High schools — Fiction.   2. Schools — Fiction.   3. Chicago (Ill.) — Fiction.]
I. Title.
PZ7.P6335Ed   1998
[Fic] — dc21   97-32332

To Gabriel Gerstenblith

THE EDUCATION OF
ROBERT NIFKIN

St. Leon's College
Parnassus on Hudson, New York

Admission Application, Page 4

64. Characterize, in essay form, your high-school ex-
    perience. You may use additional sheets of paper
    as needed.

1

My father is a son-of-a-bitch from Eastern Europe. Where he came from, getting as far as high school was a pretty big deal. He never made it. Neither did my mother, who is along similar lines to my father, although she came over when she was very young and doesn't speak with an accent. As far as my parents are concerned, when you hit high school you are an adult.

In my family, that means you are even more on your own than previously. My parents believe in the principle of "Sink or swim," or "What doesn't kill you makes you stronger—or it kills you."

So, when I hit Riverview High School, all supervision stopped, all restrictions were lifted. I could go where I wanted, stay out as late as I wanted, hang out with anybody, do anything—officially, that is. Mom and Dad were never very consistent. Any privileges could be, and were, suspended whenever they felt like it, especially my father.

When I decided I would smoke, for example, my father smacked the cigarette out of my face—and my face. This did not mean I was not allowed to smoke—just that I was not allowed to smoke cigarettes, which my father associated with men who lived off the immoral earnings of women. I was allowed to smoke cigars, however.

"Only not dem little cigars vitch also makes you look like some pimp," my father said.

Great big stogies were manly, and perfectly all right with him, and he even gave me a five-pack of Wolf Brothers Rum-Soaked Crooks to get me started right.

As a high-schooler, I was now also permitted to buy my own clothes, out of my allowance—but I could buy them only in stores my father personally approved. This meant that I could purchase trousers only at Kupferman's Pants on Roosevelt Road, and Kupferman, a friend of my father's, would sell me only one kind, blue-gray worsted wool, with pleats, and raised black twisted wiggles woven into the fabric.

"Dese are deh poifect pants for a young man in high school," Kupferman, who talks just like my father, says. "Dey vear like iron."

They also feel like iron. They make a noise when you walk, and chafe your thighs until you get used to them. You can strike matches on them.

My father gave me a brown leather briefcase, with straps, probably the only one like that in America, and a plaid scarf.

"Now you look like a sport," he said.

What I looked like was someone going to high school in maybe Lodz or Krakow, maybe twenty years ago, or my father's idea of such a person.

I forgot to mention that my father forced me to buy a pair of heavy black shoes with soles about an inch thick. They look like diver's boots and are supposed to last me the rest of my life. Which they will. Easily.

Thus, when I set out for my first day at Riverview, my appearance clearly marked me as a model geek. I was still getting used to the industrial footwear and developing the strength necessary to lift each foot. This gave me a sort of Frankenstein-monster gait. The briefcase, containing two brand-new notebooks and two Wolf Brothers Rum-Soaked Crooks cigars, bounced against my ironclad knee. I was sweating, and the extra-heavy-duty black hornrims, which my father's friend Julius the Optician had sold me, were slipping down my nose. I had the feeling—but set it down to first-day jitters—that I was about to descend into hell.

You should always trust your feelings.

II

The first thing I noticed upon entering Riverview High School was the smell. I should say smells. There was a hot steamy horrible smell that rose from the cafeteria in the basement. It was always there, at every hour of the day. It was vaguely like food of some sort. Then there was the smell of chlorine, or maybe ammonia, or maybe chlorine and ammonia, from the swimming pool, also in the basement. And the gyms were in the basement. They'd been used for a hundred years. Those were the big smells, the ones that worked their way up through the building and lingered under the roof. Mixed with them were exhaust smells from the city buses, scheduled to arrive every minute during the morning rush. They pulled up right in front of the wide bank of doors at the south end of the school, and the fumes were somehow sucked in by the opening and closing doors.

The students themselves smelled of unwashed armpit, acne cream, cheap perfume and aftershave, and stale cigarettes. Everybody smoked, right up to the door going in, and the steps outside were covered with smoldering butts.

There I stood, in the vast dark hallway, in a swirl of bluish bus exhaust, smelling the place, and noticed the second thing about the first day of school. It was chaos.

I didn't know where to go or what to do. That was to be expected—I hadn't been there for high-school-orientation day the year before—we had just moved to Chicago, my father's American hometown, during the summer—but even the kids who belonged at Riverview and had been to orientation seemed to have no idea where to go or what to do. People were asking each other where to find their homerooms; they walked in circles. People shoved each other, and banged on lockers. There was a lot of hollering. It made me dizzy.

Finally a couple of teachers showed up and shouted for new students to go into the auditorium, until they got hoarse and a couple of other teachers took their place.

I was carried along by a surge of students into the auditorium, which was huge. Little by little, it filled up with the rest of the freshmen, talking and changing their seats and yelling to friends they saw in other rows. I didn't see anyone I knew, of course, because I didn't know anybody.

It was almost as noisy in the auditorium as it had been in the hall, until Helmut Fruhling, the principal, appeared on the stage. A short, fat, bald man in a blue suit, with a broken nose and a blue chin, he was so mean-looking and scary that the kids fell silent the moment they saw him.

Helmut Fruhling leaned on the podium at the side of the stage. He gripped the corners with fat, hairy hands and growled in the microphone:

"Shuddup, students."

This was unnecessary. There wasn't a peep.

"There was some screwup, as per usual, so we will assign homerooms right now. Assistant Principal Pechvogel will read out your names and homeroom numbers. When you hear your name, get up and go."

Helmut Fruhling lurched off the stage, and Alois Pechvogel mounted the steps. He appeared to cringe when Fruhling passed him without looking at him. Pechvogel had a white rag in his hand and appeared to be polishing the handrail as he went up the steps. He polished the podium and the microphone, too.

Pechvogel was skinny and bent. He read off a paper in a cracked, nasal voice:

"Abato, Scott—228. Go! Abernathy, Louise—136. Go! Abraham, Roger—122. Go! Ackerman, Mildred—228. Go! Adams, Carol—213. Go! Adams, William—

221. Go! Adamski, Hugo—114. Go! Adanuncio, Yolanda—304. Go!"

As he read off each name, a kid would get up, thread sideways across a row, and leave the auditorium to begin looking for room 213 or 304. There were hundreds of kids. Pechvogel was reading off the names and numbers in rapid order, and it started to get hard to hear him over the shuffling of feet. Once in a while, kids would hear their names but miss the number. They'd turn to kids to the left and right and ask whether they'd heard it, or try to shout out to Mr. Pechvogel, but they were ignored.

Also, people were talking among themselves. There was a steady buzz of talk. Also, it was warm in the auditorium, and I smelled eggs. It all made me feel confused and sleepy.

Sitting next to me was a short kid with thick glasses that made his eyes look big, like something swimming in an aquarium. He had dug into a paper bag on his lap and brought out a sliced-egg sandwich, which he was eating messily.

"Isn't it exciting? We're in high school," he said, spraying me with egg.

"Lashway, Lancelot—214. Go!" Assistant Principal Pechvogel called out.

"That's me," egg-face said. "It's actually Lancelot Lashway III. Just call me Lance. I'll finish my sandwich and wait with you until you're called. Wouldn't it be

11

great if we were in the same homeroom? You want a bite of this?"

Lance Lashway held out a mangled mass of Wonder bread, mayonnaise, and bits of hard-boiled egg, which dribbled on my knees. I declined.

"What's your name?" Lance Lashway asked, wiping his hands on his shirt and offering to shake. "I'll help you listen."

"Robert Nifkin," I said, taking Lance's hand, which was fat and clammy.

"My first freshman friend in high school!" Lance said. "This is so great! You know, actually we should be called sophomores, not freshmen, 'cause this is a three-year high school and we are in tenth grade, having done ninth grade in junior high."

Assistant Principal Pechvogel droned on.

"Take a tip from me," Lance Lashway said. "Join R.O.T.C."

"What's R.O.T.C.?"

"Reserve Officers' Training Corps. It gets you ready to be a soldier. You wear a uniform on Fridays. We'll get ourselves promoted to cadet officers—then we can wear swords. Besides, if you take R.O.T.C., you don't have to take gym and get naked in front of other kids."

I pictured Lance Lashway in a uniform with a sword. He looked like a hamster. I refrained from picturing him naked.

"Nifkin, Robert—214. Go!" Pechvogel said.

"I knew it!" Lance Lashway said. "The same home-room! And you are thinking about R.O.T.C., aren't you? We're going to have a great time! Come on, cadet. Let's find our homeroom and get started on our high-school education!"

|||

The halls were full of people asking other people how to find various rooms. You might have thought the rooms would be in sequence, room 100, followed by room 101, room 102, and so on, on the first floor, 200, 201, 203 on the second floor, and the same on the third. That would make sense. But Riverview High School did not make sense. There were turns and angles and corners, passageways and bridges from one part of the building to another—and the room you were looking for could be anywhere.

Also, some staircases were for going up, and some were for going down. Hall monitors were stationed at the stairs to make sure you didn't go up a down one, or vice versa. You could get killed between classes, trying to go up stairs while a few hundred kids were thundering down—and if you tried to go down while others were going up, you'd go up.

While we searched for room 214, Lance Lashway chattered happily. It seemed he came from an old military family. His great-great-grandfather had been killed in the Civil War, his great-grandfather had been killed in the Spanish-American War, his grandfather had been killed in the First World War, and his father had been killed in World War II. He felt bad that he had not been old enough to fight in Korea, where I assume he would have been killed.

Actually, I had my doubts about Lance ever getting into the army. His glasses were as thick as hockey pucks. But he had his heart set on it, so I didn't say anything. At one point, we passed a framed picture of President Eisenhower near the main staircase, and he stopped and saluted his commander in chief. I wondered how hard it was going to be to get rid of Lance Lashway before he made me a social outcast. (I had the idea that I had a chance not to be a social outcast in my new school—or at least, if I was one, I wanted it to be my own fault, and not because I was associated with a weird, goggle-eyed, super-patriotic militarist with a death wish.)

"Look!" Lance said. "Room 214! This is it! Our homeroom! In years to come, we will always remember the good times we had here!"

We entered room 214, scene of good times to come. Behind the desk was Mrs. Kukla, a short, angry-looking woman with red-rimmed eyes.

"What's your names?" Mrs. Kukla screamed.

We told her our names. She clawed at a bunch of cards in a fiberboard box on her desk and finally came up with two stacks, one with my name at the top and one with Lance's.

"These are your program cards," she screamed. "See? There's your classes, and what room it's in, and when you go. Take these cards around to the rooms, and get the teacher to signature it in the proper place. Then come back here so I can signature your cards. If a class is full or you got a conflict, then come straight back here so I can find you a unconflicted one."

She screamed every word she said. We were back out in the hall in under a minute.

I was able to get away from Lance Lashway because we didn't have one class together. I thanked God.

These were my classes: I had English with Mrs. MacAllister, Biology with Mrs. Sweet, History with Mr. Moody, Math with Mr. Samosa, two study halls, and Gym with Coach Spline.

I found them all, and handed them my cards. All any teacher was doing today was sitting and initialing program cards. None of my new teachers bothered to look at me except Coach Spline, who was sitting at a little table in the gym, rather than at a desk.

"Give me ten laps, fatty," Coach Spline growled. He was wearing sweats and had a crew cut and a face that looked like a rotten tomato.

"Now?"

"Right now!" he bellowed, spraying me with spit. "Right now! Go! Go! Go! Go!"

I ran ten laps around the gym, wearing my street clothes and carrying my briefcase and program cards.

"Now haul your fat little butt out of here," Coach Spline said.

I hauled it.

Damp with sweat, with my hair plastered down on my head, I took my cards back to Mrs. Kukla so she could signature them.

Mrs. Kukla looked at my cards.

"Now you can get lost," Mrs. Kukla said. "Be back here first thing tomorrow morning to get indoctrinated."

I started to leave, but Mrs. Kukla called after me. "Hey, Nifkin!"

"Yes, Mrs. Kukla?"

"You don't look right to me. You're not a little goddamn Commie, by any chance?"

"Me? I'm no Communist."

"You sure? You ever hear your parents talking about Khrushchev, other than to wish him dead and in hell?"

"No, ma'am."

"Well, I'm going to keep my eye on you just the same. You don't look regular. Not a fairy, are you?"

"Not me."

"We'll see. I've got a bad feeling about you, Nifkin. I

can smell a Bolshevik a mile away—and I'm smelling one now."

Mrs. Kukla was a woman along the lines of my mother, who was also an enthusiastic anti-Communist. She was always going through my stuff, looking for subversive literature, and asking my friends whether their parents went to folk-music concerts or had any Negro friends.

I suddenly thought of something that might help get Mrs. Kukla off my back and save me from being tortured by Coach Spline.

"Mrs. Kukla, what do I have to do to take R.O.T.C. instead of Gym?"

A smile played over Mrs. Kukla's face.

"What a good idea," she said. "A little military discipline and enforced patriotism might be just what you need to get those filthy thoughts out of your head. We'll see what Sergeant Gunter can do with you. Go have him signature this card."

IV

Sergeant Gunter had short black hair with a lot of Wild-root cream oil on it, pale, dead-looking skin, and tiny black eyes. He was sitting in the R.O.T.C. room, which was in the basement. The lunchroom smell was strong in the hall outside. Inside, it was mixed with the smells of paint and floor wax. The room itself was a big empty space, with benches around the sides.

On the walls were signs, made of plywood, painted white, with careful black lettering:

> *Every citizen should be a soldier. This was the case with the Greeks and Romans, and must be that of every free state.* —THOMAS JEFFERSON

> *The Tragedy of war is that it uses Man's best to do Man's worst.* —HARRY EMERSON FOSDICK

> *Cowards can never be moral.*—MAHATMA GANDHI

Patriotism is the last refuge of a scoundrel.
—SAMUEL JOHNSON

War is hell.   —WILLIAM TECUMSEH SHERMAN

War settles nothing.   —DWIGHT D. EISENHOWER

Duty is the sublimest word in our language.
—ROBERT E. LEE

When a stupid man is doing something he is ashamed of, he always declares that it is his duty.
—GEORGE BERNARD SHAW

Duty is what one expects of others.
—OSCAR WILDE

Robert E. Lee was a weenie. —ALPHONSO GUNTER

Also on the walls were photographs of President Eisenhower and Vice-President Nixon. Under Eisenhower's picture was a card with the same black lettering as the signs: *Our Commander in Chief.*

Under Nixon's picture the card read: *Evil Weenie.*

There was an American flag in a stand and a Riverview R.O.T.C. flag at one end of the room, and a framed photograph of a bunch of sloppy-looking soldiers in odd uniforms. One of them was Sergeant Gunter. Underneath was printed: *Spain 1938*

"Welcome to Riverview High School R.O.T.C., kid," Sergeant Gunter said. "You want to join up?"

"Uh, yessir," I said.

"Yes, Sergeant," Sergeant Gunter said. "You address me as Sergeant. I am not a member of the corrupt and parasitic officer class. Why do you want to join R.O.T.C.?"

I was going to say something about it being my patriotic duty and how I always wanted to be a soldier, but for some reason I surprised myself by blurting out, "Because Coach Spline is a bastard?"

Sergeant Gunter gave me a hard look. "It is not appropriate for a cadet in Riverview High School R.O.T.C. to refer to a member of the faculty as a bastard. Give me your card. I'll sign it."

I handed him my card.

"Besides, he is not a bastard. He is a Fascist bastard. Be here at 07:15 tomorrow morning to get measured for your uniform, Nifkin."

"Yes, Sergeant," I said.

V

There I was, all enrolled. I had gotten all my cards signed, seen all my teachers, had a locker assigned and found it, located all my classrooms, been accused of being a Communist and a homosexual, and joined R.O.T.C. I'd smelled the smells, seen the students, and knew the name of another kid, even if it was Lance Lashway. I was outside in the street, and it wasn't even noon.

There were a few students coming and going, getting their programs straightened out. The weather was summery. I dug a cigar out of my briefcase and lit up on the school steps.

Next door was a place with the word *Pop's* painted on the window. I ventured in. The cigarette smoke was so thick I could hardly see. There was a smell of greasy hamburgers frying, and the place was packed with kids dancing to "Blue Suede Shoes" by Elvis Presley. It was no place to enjoy a cigar.

I found my way out of Pop's and started trudging toward home, puffing my Wolf Brothers. There was no hurry. I'd stroll, and smoke, while heading for the apartment.

My parents had found the apartment they had dreamed of for years. It was in a brand-new building. No one had ever lived in the apartment before us. They could decorate and furnish from the bare walls out and the bare floors up. They loved it. I didn't.

They had thrown themselves into the work of decorating with a sort of frenzy. They studied color schemes constantly. Every spare minute was spent visiting furniture stores. Nothing would be coming with us from the old place.

It was done in a month. The effect was stunning.

There was a lot of gilded and pickled wood, pale colors, crystal light fixtures, pastel prints, and fake-ceramic knickknacks.

"Dis is a place vould poke your eyes out," my father said.

My father could be counted on to go too far. His special contribution, made in secret at his direction, was a lamp of his own design. It was a hunk of driftwood, reaching upward with many spiky branches, stained a dark olive-brown and standing about five feet high.

There were two egg-shaped white fiberglass objects, about the size of footballs and containing lightbulbs, suspended at unequal height from the limbs. It was unpleasant to look at when switched off, and actually frightening when switched on. My mother hated it. I liked it. It was like Halloween every night of the year.

It stood there, in the corner of the living room, for months, and there was tension between my parents.

"Dis is a voik of art," my father said. And it was. It would have unnerved Dracula.

Finally, my father had it taken back to the custom-lamp maker, sprayed pink, and dusted with silver sparkles. Somewhere he found colorful little birds, made of real feathers, which he had wired to the branches.

"Before vas vinter—now is spring," he said.

My mother accepted the compromise. I had volunteered to keep the lamp, in its original tortured form, in my room, but my solution had been ignored. This was something between them, and now it was settled.

I had resisted the wallpaper with shepherdesses my mother had chosen for my bedroom. I settled for the stuff with the antique hunting scenes. I sort of liked the wall-mounted plaster bas-relief, a portrait of some eighteenth-century guy—maybe it was Mozart—my mother didn't know. I masculinized the room by keeping it as messy as possible.

Of course, the highlight was the living room, with

champagne-colored carpeting, gilt Cupids, a pickled piano that none of us could play, and a big flowery sofa covered in the finest fitted crystal vinyl. There were also transparent vinyl runners, non-yellowing, of the highest quality, laid upon the carpet and only removed when company came—on which occasions my father also put his trousers on. The rest of the time, he preferred to lounge in his boxers.

He was happy with the apartment. "I feel like a kink in his castle," he said.

Kink was right. If I ever made any friends at Riverview High School, I questioned whether it would be a good idea to let them see the French-whorehouse decor.

To my surprise, my father was back early from work. He had come upon a couple of ornaments that would give the finishing touch to the den and had hurried home to see them in place. They were full-size replicas of cellos, sort of flattened out, with the bows stuck to them, and sprayed with gold paint. He had driven picture hooks into the wall, on both sides of the couch with embroidered birds, and, with my mother's help, was hanging the second one.

"See? Dis is classy," he said. "Vit deh boids singing on deh couch is deh musical instruments. Poifect in deh den, vhere ve look on Perry Como singing on deh television. So, bum? How vas deh foist day from high school? You got in trouble yat?"

One of the reasons I am comparatively fearless is that I grew up around my father. He looks like a prize-fighter. He has a broken nose, hands like loaves of pumpernickel, and a voice—more of a growl—that makes the windows rattle. You get used to someone like that and you're hard to scare—which is not to say that I'm not scared of him.

"I joined R.O.T.C."

"Goot. Dey'll kick your ass, and make from you a man, fet little sissy."

"We're having meatlof tonight," my mother said.

I shuddered. I fear my mother's meatloaf more than I fear my father.

VI

My father likes what my mother cooks. My mother makes no pretense about her skill. She claims she was once a better cook but that making stuff my father will eat has ruined her. My father has a delicate stomach. He likes things that don't taste too much. This means that a dish might have salt *or* pepper, never both at once, and meat is cooked until it is dry and gray. What my mother does to vegetables ought to be against the law.

On a number of occasions I have asked her whether she could cook stuff for my father his way and cook stuff for me the way she used to cook. She says she has cooked for him so long that now she can't cook any other way.

Of all the tasteless, dry, horrible-looking atrocities my mother whips up in the kitchen, her meatloaf is the most depressing. You can have a better time at the dentist's than trying to eat my mother's meatloaf. A person who had just won a hundred thousand dollars in the Irish Sweepstakes, and who had never tasted my mother's meatloaf, if served the meatloaf on the day of winning the hundred thousand dollars, would be likely to commit suicide.

If there is a good side to having been raised on my mother's cooking, it is that I am unlikely to encounter anything worse. School cafeteria food is a step up. Sandwiches from a vending machine in a rest stop on the Indiana Turnpike are a step up. Mass-produced packaged imitation liverwurst in a plastic tube you can squeeze out like toothpaste is a step up. And hamburgers from Mel's are two or three steps up.

Mel's, a couple of blocks from the apartment, has the cheapest hamburgers in town. The fat-to-meat ratio is about 3 to 1, and for a dollar you can have two, in a basket with fries, a soggy pickle, and a large root beer. The airborne grease that soaks into your skin and gets on your glasses is a free extra at no additional charge, as is the vivid green pickle relish and bright yellow mustard. I visit Mel's often, especially when I have been warned that I am going to have to go through the meatloaf ordeal.

For the entire summer, Mel was about the only person in Chicago I knew by name and to talk to. Not that Mel is much for making conversation. He mostly grunts. But sometimes he drops a second pickle into my basket, which I take as a friendly gesture.

Knowing no one but Mel was only partly because we had just moved to Chicago. I had a history of being a social outcast in Quodlibet, California, before we moved. About my only friend in junior high school was Vernon Charles, the school fairy. While Vernon was willing to hang out with me on Saturdays, and come over to my house after school, he refused to let it be known we were friends, because he didn't want to ruin his reputation.

"Vernon, you're a woman!" I would say. "You read fashion magazines! And you can't afford to be seen with me?"

"I know," he would say. "I'm a little ashamed of myself for being so shallow, but, Robert, you're *really* unpopular."

I had gotten a few letters from Vernon over the summer. He'd been playing tennis with the rich popular kids and was thinking of running for freshman class president at Quodlibet High School. Vernon is a social butterfly.

I am a social slug.

So being on my own in Chicago wasn't that much of a change, and Chicago was a lot more interesting than Quodlibet. For part of the summer, while my father got used to his new job and my mother looked for an apartment, we had lived in the Harbor Hotel. This was great, because my mother couldn't do any cooking there and I had all my meals at the counter in the drugstore downstairs.

I was free to wander around and explore the city. I liked it right away. Quodlibet is sort of a suburb, with nothing in it but houses and a few boring stores.

Chicago is like an enormous amusement park—better, because everything is real. The first thing I liked about it, and still like, was the architecture. Big buildings are indescribably cool. The old skyscrapers have all kinds of ornaments and surprising shapes. The modern ones are taller and bigger, with wild-looking spaces inside. I liked the different colors and textures of the buildings, and the different ways they look at different times of day. What makes it all even better is that people are constantly going in and out of the buildings, moving through the spaces, through the streets—and I could, too.

People walk fast in Chicago, and I learned to move through the pedestrian traffic, avoiding collisions, changing lanes, going into the lobbies of buildings, moving through the crowds of people and out through another door. It was like a ride. My legs would carry me smoothly, as though I were on rails, and I'd move swiftly through the Loop—that's downtown, where all the big buildings are. After a while, all the empty space, between and inside the buildings, and all the solid space—the buildings themselves, cars, buses, people— would start to feel like it was all moving, dancing. It was like music. I still love to do this. I'll never get tired of it.

Away from the Loop, the buildings are smaller, but they can be interesting in different ways. Different neighborhoods have different looks, and you never have to go far before coming upon something amazing—a church, a building with sculptures in front, a house that looks like an old farmhouse, or one that looks like something someplace in Europe, a castle built hundreds of years ago. And there's more! There are parks and trees, and the whole place is spread out along the shore of the lake, so you can step out of this fantastic thing made up of buildings and all of a sudden you're in someplace green, with trees, and looking at blue water that goes to the horizon. And just to make it more magical, the parks have statues in them, so you're walking along and all of a sudden you're involved with this big sculpture of Abraham Lincoln or some other fascinating surprise.

And any time you like, while speeding on foot through all this incredible stuff, you can stop and get a Chicago-type hot dog with everything. They sell them all over the place. And everything includes green relish, yellow mustard, chopped onions, tomatoes, hot peppers, a pickle spear—in other words, everything.

When I got tired of touring the city on foot, I would drop into cheap movie houses to catch a double feature and enjoy the air conditioning. My favorite was the Clark, which had two different movies every day, old ones I'd never heard of and movies made in foreign countries. I saw *Dracula, The Mummy, M, Seven Samurai, The Lavender Hill Mob, Sunrise,* and *Grand Illusion,* all good movies.

I also discovered the main branch of the Chicago Public Library, the inside of which is all white marble covered with brightly colored mosaics. It's a nice place to read, and I also checked out books. Sometimes I would take my book to the mezzanine of the Palmer House hotel and sit in one of the big easy chairs and have a cigar while I read.

In Grant Park, beside the lake, right across from the Loop, there's this huge semicircular concrete thing, looking like half a loudspeaker, and big enough for a symphony orchestra to sit inside it. It works like a loudspeaker, too. They have free concerts there. I went to one.

And there is a zoo in Lincoln Park. I hit the zoo just about every day. I can't say which animals are my favorites, I enjoy watching them all, but the Siberian tigers and the gorillas are pretty wonderful, and the zoo is another good place to enjoy a Wolf Brothers Rum-Soaked Crook, plus you can get fresh-roasted peanuts.

I have not seen Paris or Rome or any of those places, but I don't see how Chicago can be improved on.

VII

So there I was, on the afternoon of my first day of high school, about to fill up with Melburgers in preparation for being once again exposed to my mother's dreaded meatloaf. Mel was puttering behind his counter, listening to the staticky radio, the industrial floor-model fan was making the dust-and-grease icicles that hung from the ceiling dance and sway, and my glasses were slowly clouding up with the tiny grease droplets that floated in the air. My favorite counter stool rocked and creaked. It was homey and familiar.

About two stools down from me, at the end of the counter, sat a female. This was unusual. Girls and women don't patronize Mel's much. It's mostly men in steel-toed work shoes. I suppose the women don't like the smell of hamburger grease in their hair, or they believe more in the germ theory, or don't want to get fat—anyway, they don't show up much.

This female was a girl around my age. She was short and blond, and sort of lumpy-looking. She was nibbling at a double triple with cheese. A triple is three fatburger patties on a bun, and obviously a double triple is two of them. Even I am afraid of a triple. Only polar bears and Arctic wolves can digest them. Here was this mere slip of a lump of a girl, in her oversized Riverview basketball jacket, gnawing away with her little lipsticked mouth, dabbing daintily at the grease on her chin with a napkin. I noticed that her nail polish was chipped, and she had Band-Aids on three knuckles of one hand and two knuckles of the other.

She noticed me at the same time I noticed her. She looked at the Band-Aids.

"I was punching out a girl at Pop's earlier," she said. "The bitch was making moves on my boyfriend, Kenny Papescu. You know him?"

"Can't say that I do," I said.

"He comes in here sometimes. Tall guy with thick glasses and a big nose. Curly hair. Walks like an ape."

"I may have seen him around," I said.

"He's my sweetie."

The girl wiped a hand on her calf-length black skirt, held it out to me.

"Linda Pudovkin. Don't get any ideas."

"I'm Robert Nifkin," I said, taking her small, still-greasy hand.

Linda Pudovkin was working a piece of gristle from

between her teeth with a pinky nail. "My parents are divorced. My father is a psychiatrist. He's racked with guilt. Gives me all the money I want."

I couldn't tell if she was complaining or bragging.

"That's interesting," I said.

"You're a freshman at Riverview, right?" she asked.

"Yes. How about you?"

"Technically, no," Linda Pudovkin said. "But since I failed everything last year, I'm taking all freshman courses over again."

"You failed everything?"

"My father is frantic. If I pass this year, he's going to let me go to Paris this summer, and take Kenny with me."

"Cool."

"Of course, we won't come back. We'll live on the Left Bank and be poets or something."

Linda Pudovkin abruptly stood up, took a last swig of her root beer, and headed for the door.

"I'll tell Kenny I met you. He doesn't go to Riverview. He doesn't go to school at all, but his parents don't know that. Be nice to him—he's got a car."

She slammed the screen door on her way out.

Mel brought me my double single. As usual, my French fries were only about three-quarters cooked and my root beer was flat. You get perfect consistency at Mel's—it's one of the signs of a professionally run restaurant.

"You know that girl?" I asked Mel.

"Linda? I've known her all her life. Her father is a great psychiatrist. If it weren't for him, I wouldn't be where I am today. Oh, look! There's that goddamn mouse! I've been after him all day. Hold still, you little bastard!"

Mel went after the mouse with a broom. Mel was whacking the floor where the mouse had been, but the mouse was long gone. I'd seen it all before.

I tucked into my first burger. Mel had dumped about a cup of salt on the French fries, which did not take away from their being raw in the middle—but over the weeks, I had become able to digest them.

A tall kid whose head of curly hair had corners, wearing two-tone glasses, came in. His nose looked like one of those joke noses that come with glasses attached, and he had a sort of staring expression that made him look like something carved of wood.

"You Robert?" the tall kid asked.

I nodded.

"I'm double-parked. You can bring the burgers with you. You going to eat both of those?"

"Please, help yourself," I said as I followed him out of Mel's carrying my double single and my paper container of root beer.

"Thanks," the tall kid said, and, "Get in."

With one of my hamburgers, he gestured to a rusty Plymouth station wagon with the motor running, making smoke in the middle of the street.

"You're Kenny Papescu, right?" I asked him.

"Linda sent me," Kenny Papescu replied.

VIIII

"Where are we going?" I asked Kenny Papescu.

"Move a desk. You get five bucks."

"I have to be back for supper."

"No problem. It'll just take twenty minutes."

Kenny was driving with one hand and finishing off my fatburger. He whipped the big station wagon around corners and made the tires squeal.

"Linda is some beautiful babe, huh?" he asked me.

"Sure. Beautiful."

"Don't get any ideas."

"I know. She told me."

"We're there. Come on."

Kenny had parked the station wagon in an alley. We went into the service entrance of some building and got into a freight elevator. Kenny started it by reaching through a hole in the side and pulling on a cable. It rose slowly. He stopped it by pulling on the cable the other way, and opened the door, which was sort of like a garage door.

We stepped out into a big room, dark, with a few bare lightbulbs dangling from the ceiling, making little puddles of light.

"Here it is," Kenny said.

It was something fairly large and as high as my chin, covered with a piece of canvas with ropes tied around it.

"You're strong, right?" Kenny asked me.

"Pretty strong."

"Good, 'cause this thing is heavy. It's made of African rosewood."

We wrestled the object onto the elevator. It *was* heavy.

"Wait until you see this," Kenny Papescu said. "It was made in Turkey or someplace. It has carving and ivory and ebony inlays all over it. Must be worth a few thousand. Whatever you do, don't drop your end—my father and Linda's father will kill my ass if we damage it."

In the alley we wrestled the thing into the station wagon. We had to turn it on its side, and it just fit. Then we jumped into the car, and Kenny gunned the engine.

"Okay. Now to deliver it."

"What is it exactly?"

"Desk. Really fancy roll-top desk. We're taking it to

Linda's father. He thinks it belonged to Sigmund Freud."

"Did it?"

"No. My father told him that. Well, we don't know that it *didn't* belong to Sigmund Freud. I suppose it could have. Anyway, it belonged to somebody pretty important—you just have to look at it. Could have belonged to a king or something. Wait until you see it."

Kenny careened the station wagon into another alley. We had more trouble getting the desk out of the back of the station wagon than we'd had getting it in. Then we moved it through a door with a lot of garbage cans standing around and directly into a grimy storeroom. I smelled cooking and coffee. I could see we were in the back room of some kind of deli or luncheonette.

"Dr. Pudovkin," Kenny yelled. "We brought it!"

A very large, very fat man in a pinstripe suit appeared from the public part of the restaurant, pulled a key ring from his pocket, and unlocked a door.

"Bring it in here, boys," he said.

We moved the desk through the door, into a very fancy room, with leather chairs, oil paintings on the walls, and thick carpet. There was a big leather couch, and a smell I'd never smelled, but I knew it must be really good cigars.

"Put it right here," Dr. Pudovkin said.

We wrestled the desk into place, and Kenny untied

the ropes and removed the canvas, which he made into a bundle and held in his arms.

It was *some* desk, carved all over, with black-and-white designs inlaid and carved ivory knobs on the drawers. The wood was reddish and dark, and gleamed richly.

"Wow! Tell your father he did a great job," Dr. Pudovkin said. "The thing looks just beautiful."

"It sure does, Doc," Kenny said.

Dr. Pudovkin dug two ten-dollar bills out of his pocket and gave us each one. Then he put his arm around Kenny's shoulder and sort of half-whispered in his ear, "Kenny, I wish you'd think about joining the navy or something and leaving my daughter alone."

"I love Linda, Dr. Pudovkin," Kenny said.

"I know you do," Dr. Pudovkin said. "But wouldn't you like to go to Hollywood? You're a handsome boy—maybe you could get work acting in the movies. I'd be happy to get you started."

"Naw. I want to go to Paris with Linda next summer, like you promised."

Dr. Pudovkin patted Kenny on the back. "Yes, yes, but just think about it. You'd make me so happy if you'd go away. Want to see Australia? It's a wonderful place."

"I don't think so," Kenny said.

"Give my regards to your father," Dr. Pudovkin said.

Kenny and I got back into the station wagon and weaved through traffic.

"Dr. Pudovkin sure wants to get rid of you," I said.

"Yeh. He's a nice guy. It's like knives in his heart to think I could be his son-in-law someday."

We pulled up in front of my apartment house. Kenny handed me a five-dollar bill.

"Pudovkin gave me ten," I said.

"That was a tip. You made fifteen, man," Kenny said. "See ya."

He roared away, making black exhaust smoke.

IX

07:15. That's a quarter past seven in the morning. I got to see my fellow R.O.T.C. cadets. Lance Lashway was there, of course, glowing with happiness. It didn't take a minute to see why these guys had joined. It was like the Bad Posture Club. People slouched, slumped, walked with their toes pointed in, didn't move their arms when they walked, had potbellies, big bottoms, knock-knees, were real fat, real thin, real tall, and real short—in other words, everybody there had a good reason not to want to get undressed in front of other kids in the gym locker room. I also understood what uniforms were for—to try to hide how completely funny-looking most humans are.

But the uniforms couldn't hide the pimply, pale, openmouthed, drooling, unintelligent, abnormal, un-comprehending faces. Lance Lashway was an outstanding specimen of young manhood in this group. And I belonged to this group. It was depressing to think about.

We were lined up in ranks, and the cadet officers tried to teach us right-face, left-face, and parade rest. A lot of people had big problems with right and left. One by one, we were called out of line and into the storeroom, where Sergeant Gunter and three or four senior cadets issued us our uniforms. Sergeant Gunter had a tape measure around his neck, and would measure each kid, and call out the sizes to the cadets, who would pull the uniforms off shelves. We each got a cap, a jacket, a shirt, a tie, a belt, and trousers, also a brass cap badge, a brass lapel insignia, and a book that told how to wear the uniform and take care of it. We had to supply our own shoes, socks, and underwear.

In my case, there was no uniform. I am a person of size, as I prefer to say, and it seems I qualified for the maximum army suit made, but not kept in stock by Riverview R.O.T.C. Sergeant Gunter said he would have to request one from the Quartermaster Department, and it would be shipped out. If they didn't have one on hand, they would make me one. This pleased me. All the other kids were being issued hand-me-down, used uniforms in which other kids had sweated and farted. I was getting a brand-new one. Moreover, as an un-uniformed cadet, I would not be associated right away with my ugly, awkward, stupid-looking comrades-in-arms. Sergeant Gunter said it might take a few weeks until my uniform arrived. I told him I didn't mind.

After everyone but me had been given a uniform, we were sent back into the R.O.T.C. room, to sit on benches, while cadet officers told us how to wear the uniform, where to place the insignia, and so forth— the same stuff that was in the book. We were required to wear the uniforms to school every Friday. For the rest of the next week, we had classes about nothing but how to wear the uniform, how many inches, and fractions, from the edge of the lapel to pin the brass insignia, the way to put the cap on at the correct angle, how to tie a tie, how to polish the brass buttons—and still on the first Friday, when everybody but me would come to school in uniform, and the second, and the third, some kids would have their caps on sideways, their ties knotted bizarrely and insignia upside down.

We sat in the R.O.T.C. room until the bell rang to start school, being told and shown over and over how to pin the badge on our cap. The boredom turned into mental pain, and the mental pain turned into physical pain, and then my brain turned off and I could feel nothing. I just sat there, feeling the warmth of the other kids on the benches and smelling the mothball smell of the uniforms. After a while, Sergeant Gunter came out of the storeroom and said that what we were experiencing was exactly like the real army.

X

Homeroom. Room 214. Mrs. Kukla yelled a little speech at the top of her lungs.

"This is your homeroom which it's the place you come first every day. If any of your teachers wants to make a complaint about you it comes here. I don't want to have to signature any complaint cards, so watch your p's and q's. Some of you students will have me for English as your English teacher and I will have you as students. You will find that I am a fair teacher, and I hope you will all turn out to be a fair student. I am not asking anybody to like me, and I am not asking to like you, but I want to ask you that we all try to like each other because we're stuck. So if you have a problem, tell me about them.

"Today only, and not tomorrow, you will return to this room at the end of the day. If you have any questions, that will be the time to ask it, because I am not only here to create answers, I am also here to create your problem. This way we can be creative at Riverview High School.

"I want you to pass quietly through the halls, learn the rules of Riverview High School, and think of me as your homeroom teacher.

"One more thing. If anybody gives you Communist propaganda or pornography, I want to see it. I hope you will all enjoy your studentship here at our school."

The bell rang, and we all went out into the busy halls to begin our studentship.

I made my way to my first class. It was English with Mrs. MacAllister. She was a nice-looking, white-haired lady. I found a seat in the back. Mrs. MacAllister smiled sweetly at us.

"Children, now that you are in high school, and on your way to becoming young adults and citizens, you need to understand some very important things that are happening in our world. I know you are fine young people, and want to live decent lives, and one day embark on careers, raise families, make your parents and your school proud of you, and be good Americans and good Christians.

"Some of you have been taught at home or in church—but others of you may not know—that there are people who do not want us to have a fine country, with honest citizens and decent standards, in which we can all be proud to live. These people are the Jews."

I *had* been taught about this at home. I had heard my father mention anti-Semites, but this was the first time I had ever seen one. I was fascinated. Mrs. Kukla was phobic about Communists and homosexuals, but Mrs. MacAllister left her miles behind. She went on, still with the sweet smile.

"I know we have Jewish students in this school. We are obliged to have them—it is the law—and I want it understood that I have nothing against them personally. Children should not be held responsible for the misdeeds of their parents, and every one of us is free to reject evil and accept the Christian faith or, for the less intelligent, Catholicism. But it is my duty to tell you that, for centuries, the Jews have been getting in everywhere, and their goal is to destroy society.

"They are terribly clever, you see. They will appear to be ordinary people, like us, but they are not. Jews all over the world are part of a vast secret organization, an international conspiracy. They control the banks, and all the money in the world. They are the people behind the World Communist Movement. And Jews want to destroy our traditional values. They are sexual deviants, and they spread pornography."

I saw she was not all that distant from Mrs. Kukla, just a little crazier, and classier. It was better as a sort of all-in-one conspiracy with the evil Jews behind it.

"So, if any of the Jewish students try to indoctrinate you, offer you any literature or pornographic materials,

I hope you will report it to me at once, for their own good as well as yours."

We were on familiar ground. It was just the same as what Mrs. Kukla had said, and except that she was Jewish herself, my mother would have agreed with every word. I wondered where these women had gotten the stuff about the propaganda and the pornography being handed around. Did they read about it in some secret paper? Was there an international crazy-ladies conspiracy?

Mrs. MacAllister finished warning us about Jews, and we spent the rest of the period copying into our notebooks that which she had written on the board in extremely neat and legible script:

Icelandic Literature. Early Icelandic literature emerged in the 13th century from the oral tradition of Eddic and skaldic poetry, both of which were based on ancient Icelandic mythology. Other early writings (14th–16th centuries) include sagas of Norse monarchs, translations of foreign romances, and religious works. From the 14th–19th centuries the rímur, narrative verse poems, were popular. The 19th century was probably the most important period in the development of Icelandic literature. Romantic lyric poets such as Bjarni Thorarensen and Jónas Hallgrímsson were influential in stimulating literary activity. Other figures were Jón Thóroddsen, who published the first novel in Icelandic, and Matthías Jochumsson, the founder of modern Icelandic drama. The late 19th century saw the development of Icelandic realism.

Important 20th-century writers include Gunnar Gunnarsson and Halldór Laxness.

And so on.

We never did get to read any of this stuff, or any of the stuff she would write about on the board. We just copied it into our notebooks and were graded on the notebooks at the end of the semester.

XI

After Mrs. MacAllister's English class, I went to the R.O.T.C. room for my scheduled class time there. (The before-school stuff was just to get issued uniforms and, later, for marching practice, which was optional, only you could not get promoted to a higher rank unless you attended the early-morning sessions, which I never did, which is why I never was.)

It was more of how to put your cap on, how to tie your tie, how to pin the insignia on, how to salute. I was already learning the technique of open-eyed napping. Sergeant Gunter was impressive as he conducted the lecture while asleep himself.

In between dozing, I thought about Mrs. MacAllister and wondered how many more like her there were. We had beaten the Nazis in Europe just a few years earlier, and I guessed that sort of thinking had probably been unpopular while we were fighting them, but there was Mrs. MacAllister, big as life, teaching her classes to be Jew haters.

I was learning a lot on my first day.

I would have bet that nothing could top Mrs. Kukla and Mrs. MacAllister, but I had not yet been to Miss Sweet's Biology class.

It came next.

Miss Sweet was obviously crazy. You could see that just by looking at her. Her white hair was wild, half the buttons on her clothes were undone or buttoned to the wrong buttonhole, she moved like a person in a dream, and she had a wild, half-staring, half-smiling expression. The Biology room was crowded with dirty glass cases and aquariums full of plant life. In one tank there was an alligator, about two feet long. The light that made it through the windows was green and dim because of all the ferns and other plants on the windowsills. There was a smell of rotting vegetation, and the walls were damp.

Miss Sweet spoke in a tiny voice, like a little girl. She didn't talk to us. Maybe she was talking to God.

"Why? Why do they keep sending children here? How can I take care of all my plants, and the alligator, when they keep sending these children here? Oh, where am I supposed to put them? I don't know anything about children."

She was rushing back and forth, twisting her hands. It was scary and pathetic. There was a freestanding wooden wardrobe near the front of the room. All the classrooms had them. They were used as coat closets by the teachers. Miss Sweet actually climbed into hers and pulled the door closed after her. We could hear her babbling and moaning inside.

It was very uncomfortable. We quietly took seats. On the blackboard there was stuff written. We took out our notebooks and copied it down.

Mold, any of a wide variety of tiny fungi that form furry growths on food, leather, textiles, and other organic materials in moist environments. Some molds, including Aspergillum and Penicillium, are important in cheese-making or as sources of antibiotics and some organic chemicals. Like other fungi, molds cannot make their own food by photosynthesis. They are generally saprophytes that obtain their food by assisting in the decay of the organic materials on which they grow. The "body" of a mold, called the mycelium, consists of a network of fine filaments through which nutrients are absorbed. Molds reproduce by means of spores produced in spore cases or other reproductive structures that give molds their characteristic black, blue, green, orange, or red colors. Most familiar molds are members of the orders Mucorales and Eurotiales.

"Copy the pictures of the mold spores, children," Miss Sweet called from inside the wardrobe.

We copied them.

Then the bell rang, and we quietly filed out.

XII

Lunchtime at Riverview High School proved to be all I anticipated, and more. The lunchroom was crowded on the first day of school. In a few days, the number of regular lunchroom lunchers would thin out, as students found nearby cheap-food stands, or brought bag lunches from home, or did without rather than try to eat the Riverview food. I, of course, liked the cooking, which was lots nicer than my mother's.

I had found a seat out of Lance Lashway's line of sight. He was sitting at a long table with a bunch of R.O.T.C. guys. I was being careful to avoid Lance Lashway. Being seen in his company, right at the beginning of things, could mean Quodlibet, California, all over again. I was just thinking this, when he stood up and led the other R.O.T.C. cadets in a song from *The Student Prince*. They waved their individual containers of chocolate milk in unison as they sang. I crouched down in my chair.

"My father says you're potentially normal."

I looked up sideways. Doing so, I realized that I was sitting with my eyes just above the level of the table. Linda Pudovkin was standing over me, holding a tray.

"Mind if I join you?"

This was sophisticated, and had never happened before—a girl was going to eat lunch with me.

"Not at all. Please be seated," I said, handling it extremely well. I rose partially out of my seat and gestured to a chair. At that moment Lance Lashway saw me, smiled, and raised his milk carton in salute. I pretended I hadn't seen him.

Linda took the place opposite mine. I noted that she, too, had selected the mashed potatoes and gravy and bread—the same as myself, and also the chocolate milk.

"What is it with your father?" I asked Linda. "He's got what looks like an office in the back of what looks like a luncheonette."

"It *is* his office," Linda said. "We think he also sleeps there—we're not sure. Since the divorce—to economize, I guess—he has a deal with the owner of the place, or maybe he owns it with him. He sees patients there, mostly at one of the tables."

"It just seemed a little weird," I said.

"It is—and he is," Linda said. "And of course he eats continuously. My mother says she always thought what he needed instead of a wife was a short-order cook, and now he's got one."

"I hope you don't mind that I asked you a personal question," I said.

"Not at all. And speaking of personal—be informed that I will report this whole conversation to Kenny Papescu, so count your words. Anything out of line and you will have to defend yourself."

"I understand," I said. "Kenny Papescu is fiercely jealous."

"We both are. It comes of being frustrated, I think. While we are almost always together, we have decided to remain virgins."

"Until you're married," I said.

"Or even after," Linda said. "When we need to overcome desire, we talk on the phone while wearing boxer shorts on our heads—which does the trick. You might keep it in mind."

"Thanks. I will."

At this point Lance Lashway and the R.O.T.C. boys broke into a song in German, and most of the kids in the lunchroom joined in.

"Do you ever get the feeling you're in a black-and-white movie?" I asked Linda.

"All the time," she said.

XIII

After lunch—History with Mr. Moody. I could hardly wait to see what he had to offer. He did not disappoint me. Mr. Moody had red hair and a reddish complexion. The rims of his eyes were red, too. He wore a rumpled blue suit with smears of cigarette ash on it, and his shoes were scuffed.

"I just want you all to know I could make three times as much in industry. People like me are in demand in industry. I could walk out of here and get an executive-trainee position tomorrow. Look at this crappy suit! This is what you can buy on a teacher's pay. I am a graduate of the University of Illinois. I don't have to teach!

"Six years ago, I was in Germany with the peace-time army, protecting this country against Communism. I got a lousy deal in the army. They don't have due process like we do in civilian life. Some officer doesn't like you, he can accuse you of anything, and you're guilty until proven innocent. I teach because I want to. It's a calling, like a priest. I could get a job with Motorola, or some other big company—start at three times what I get now, live in the suburbs, have a new car.

"And does anybody give me any respect? When you're a teacher you're like dirt under everybody's feet. They assume you're a failure because you chose this profession—and it is a profession, don't make any mistake about that, boys and girls. It's a calling, like a priest.

"I risked my life in postwar Germany to protect our way of life, and I am dedicated to the teaching profession. I could have taken a business course and been sitting pretty by now. I made plenty of sacrifices, and for who? For you, that's who! So I can guide you and teach you, and you can go to college, and study management or accounting, and get that cushy job and live in the suburbs.

"Therefore, I do not have to take any crap from you kids. I don't want to hear any excuses, I don't want any problems, and I don't want any fooling around in class. After class, if you see me in the pool hall, that's a different story. Mr. Moody is a regular guy. Anybody will tell you Mr. Moody is a regular guy. You want to shoot a game of pool with Mr. Moody, that's fine. But not here. We are here to work.

"Now copy this stuff off the board. It goes in your permanent notebook, which will account for seventy-five percent of your grade. May as well get started learning this stuff right now, okay?"

Stephen Grover Cleveland was born in 1837, in Caldwell, N.J., and died in 1908. He was the 22nd and 24th President of the United States. In 1886 he married Frances Folsom; they had five children. A lawyer in Buffalo, N.Y., Cleveland was elected mayor of that city in 1881. His reputation as a reformer led to his nomination and election as Democratic governor of New York. He quickly achieved a national reputation, and the Democrats chose him as their presidential candidate in 1884. He won a narrow victory over James G. Blaine.

His first term was marked by an attempt to reform the civil service and by his advocacy of a low tariff; both issues had strong opponents in both parties. He ran for re-election in 1888 but was narrowly defeated by Benjamin Harrison, the Republican candidate and an advocate of a high tariff.

In 1892, he was nominated again, and this time he decisively defeated Harrison. The Panic of 1893 raised the issue of free coinage of silver, which was supported by the radical or free-silver Democrats. An economic conservative, Cleveland opposed free coinage and secured the repeal of the Sherman Silver Purchase Act, which enraged the radical Democrats. In 1894, he broke the Pullman Strike in Chicago by the use of federal troops. The free-silver Democrats prevailed at the 1896 convention and nominated William Jennings Bryan.

He was essentially a moderate in foreign policy. Cleveland broadened the interpretation of the Monroe Doctrine in the Venezuela Boundary Dispute with Great Britain. He refused to annex Hawaii after a U.S.–backed faction overthrew the monarchy, and he discouraged those who wanted to take Cuba from Spain.

It was evident that the whole school worked on the notebook system. Mr. Moody was clearly more serious than Mrs. MacAllister and Miss Sweet—he gave us lots more to copy off the board. And no mention of Jews or pornography as yet. After Sergeant Gunter, Mr. Moody was my favorite teacher so far.

XIV

I had seen *The Mummy* with Boris Karloff at the Clark Theater during the summer. I had seen it twice, in fact. This prepared me for Mr. Samosa, the Math teacher. Mr. Samosa was almost silent. When he did speak, he whispered. He hardly moved. He wore a black suit. His eyes appeared to be half-closed—he never looked at you.

"Take seats. Copy what's on the board," Mr. Samosa said, almost inaudibly.

I had wondered, but only for a second on the way in, how Math could be taught using the Riverview notebook system.

Mathematics: study concerned originally with the properties of numbers and space; now more generally concerned with deductions made from assumptions about abstract entities. Mathematics is often divided into applied mathematics, which involves the use of mathematical reasoning in engineering, physics, chemistry, economics, etc., and pure mathematics, which is purely abstract reasoning based on axioms. However, the two fields are not totally independent—the subjects of pure mathematics are often chosen for their application to specific problems, and the abstract results of pure mathematics, such as group theory and differential geometry, often find practical uses. The main divisions of pure mathematics are into geometry and algebra. Often analysis, reasoning using the concept of limits, is distinguished from algebra; it includes the differential and integral calculus.

All we could hear was the sound of ballpoints on notebook paper, and our own quiet breathing. When the bell rang, we jumped.

I then proceeded to two study halls, back-to-back. It was the only time I would show up for study hall. Sitting across the aisle from me was a good-natured fellow named Neil. Neil had the sleeves of his T-shirt rolled way up and wore a crude, homemade tattoo, which read:

BORN ᵀᴼ A LOSE

He was working on a tattoo on the arm of a girl with curlers in her hair who sat in front of him. She was twisted around in her seat, so her arm lay across Neil's desk. Neil poked and scratched at her arm with an open safety pin, and then dripped ink from a fountain pen onto the place he'd scratched, wiped the excess ink away with a Kleenex, and scratched some more. Her tattoo read:

KEVN

I guess Kevn was her boyfriend.

"Hey! Kid!" Neil whispered to me. "When they pass the card back, next to your name write 'Band Practice.' "

"Why?" I asked him.

"That way you're excused from study hall. Whoever's the study-hall teacher won't report you absent, 'cause you have band practice, and the band teacher won't report you absent because he never heard of you."

Neil collapsed in snorts and giggles.

I looked around the study hall, which was like a vast classroom, with row after row of seats bolted to the floor. People were reading newspapers, a few read paperback books, some were sleeping, some were eating, the kid in the seat to my left was spitting on his desk and mixing the spit with ink. Nobody was studying.

When the card with spaces to be signed by every person in my row was handed back to me, I signed my name and wrote "Band Practice."

Neil wrote "Band Practce."

With nothing following study hall, except another study hall, which I would also convert to band practice, this meant that I'd be clear of the school every day at

2:15—except today. Today I had to sit through both study halls. I watched Neil work on the "Kevn" tattoo, and watched the kid opposite play with his spit. The girl in the curlers, who was getting the tattoo, popped her bubblegum, and now and then rolled her eyes at me and said, "Oooo, it hurts."

"But think how pleased Kevn will be," I said.

"Yeh," she said.

The bell rang at last, and I made my way to room 214.

Mrs. Kukla had some last words for us on our first day.

"You are real high-schoolers now. Come back tomorrow, all of you, and keep your nose clean."

XV

"So, bum. How is by you deh education?" My father was sucking up his favorite mashed-eggplant dish, made without spices by my mother. This is one I have flatly refused to try. Another of his favorites, which I tried once, and never again, is cold beet borscht with sour cream. It's not so much the way these things taste that nauseates me, it's the way they look, especially when my father eats them. My father is a messy eater. He sprays food when he talks, and sort of throws it around. He gets hunks of eggplant on his face, or pieces of chicken, or (specially disgusting) jellied calves' feet. He even gets food on his forehead. When he gets up from the table, my mother has to vacuum. He leaves a circle of debris, such as you might find around a parrot's cage. The weird thing is that he never messes up his clothes. He is always crisp and neat. At the end of a long day, he looks like he just got dressed—his shirt is fresh and white, his pants sharply creased, no dust on his shiny black shoes.

"I don't know, Dad. I think it's a crappy school."

"Oh? Awlready you're an expert? You know more than deh teachers? Dey should make you principal, maybe?"

"It looks like all we do is read stuff off the blackboard and copy it into our notebooks. So far nobody has explained anything."

"So? Reading? Writing? Vhat else you vant? It sounds fine to me. In Europe, I valked six miles troo deh snow to deh school, and in dose days dere vas volfs. Mine own brudder, a volf came along and bit a piece out from him, and he still had to sit in deh school deh whole day, and deh teacher gave him a big hit in the head for complaining. You should be grateful you get to go to a fine school."

"Yes, Dad."

"On deh vay home, deh volf bit him anudder time, just for good measure, and vhen ve came home, deh momma gave us a big hit in the head for being late. And vhen deh poppa came home, he gave us a big hit in deh head, because he always did. And dis vas a *good* day."

My mother was smoking cigarettes between bites, as usual. "What your father is trying to tell you, in his quaint Old World way, is that nobody likes a complainer," she said. "Just do your best, and keep your nose clean. You're not hanging around with any Communists, are you? You haven't been asked to go to any meetings?"

"Not so far," I said.

"Just remember, those Reds are always on the lookout for a simpleminded kid like you, without any friends. If anybody starts in being nice to you, it's safe to assume they're trying to recruit you for the Party."

"Okay, Mom."

"That's my good boy. I made bread pudding with raisins for dessert."

"Goody."

Another standard mealtime in our apartment. After supper my parents went into the den, to sit on the couch with the birds and watch TV, and I went to my bedroom, to try to tune in *The Goon Show* on my Hallicrafters shortwave receiver.

XVI

The next day of classes at Riverview High School was pretty much identical to the first. Mrs. Kukla yelled at us and told us to keep our noses clean. Mrs. MacAllister told us more about the International Jewish Communist Bankers Conspiracy, and had us copy stuff off the board about Old Norse literature, which is mainly mythological poetry and sagas, recorded in Eddic and skaldic Icelandic verse, whatever those are. We watched Miss Sweet, lost in her dim green world of madness, rushing up and down, carrying on a conversation with herself, or someone only she could see.

In R.O.T.C., Cadet Captain Engelhardt, a senior, continued to prepare everybody but me for wearing the uniform come Friday, going over the same details about cap angle and badge placement, again and again. When he asked the kids sitting on benches to repeat what he had just said, most of them got it wrong, or couldn't remember any of it.

Sergeant Gunter had a desk in the storeroom. We could see him through the open door, reading a book which he had covered with brown wrapping paper. Now and then he would walk into the R.O.T.C. room and read aloud to us.

The bourgeoisie, by the rapid improvement of all instruments of production, by the immensely facilitated means of communication, draws all nations, even the most barbarian, into civilization. The cheap prices of its commodities are the heavy artillery with which it batters down all Chinese walls, with which it forces the barbarians' intensely obstinate hatred of foreigners to capitulate. It compels all nations, on pain of extinction, to adopt the bourgeois mode of production; it compels them to introduce what it calls civilization into their midst, i.e., to become bourgeois themselves. In a word, it creates a world after its own image.

Then he would go back to his desk, and Cadet Captain Engelhardt would tell us again how the bottom right edge of the cap should rest two fingers' width above the right eyebrow. And after a while Sergeant Gunter would come out and read to us some more.

Of all the classes that stand face-to-face with the bourgeoisie today, the proletariat alone is a really revolutionary class. The other classes decay and finally disappear in the face of modern industry; the proletariat is its special and essential product.

At lunch, in the noisy, steamy, underground lunch-room, I looked around for Linda Pudovkin, but didn't see her. I took my tray with the mashed potatoes and gravy and bread and chocolate milk to a completely empty table and sat down. Within one minute, all the other chairs were occupied with kids who were very fat, or very thin, or had thick glasses, or wore dumb-looking clothes, or twitched, or smelled, or lisped, or shrieked, or had horrible acne, or weird haircuts, or frightening-looking braces, or slide rules clipped to their belts, or all of the above. I had found the geek table. I looked around. My fellow lunchers smiled brightly at me. I sighed, and dug into my lumpy mashed potatoes. I was where I belonged.

The kid sitting to my right was wearing a cowboy shirt, buttoned up to the neck. It had a cowboy on a rearing horse above each pocket.

"Hello. My name is Detleff. I am a refugee from Europe," the kid said.

I told him my name.

"My father does not use a handkerchief to clean his glasses," Detleff said. "Can you guess how he cleans them?"

"Not really," I said.

"He uses his fingers!" Detleff said. "It is a good trick. I will show you."

Detleff removed his grimy glasses and rubbed the

lenses between his thumb and fingers, and put them back on. They looked smeary and greasy.

"You see? You can clean your glasses without a handkerchief. This is a good trick, yes?"

"Great, Detleff," I said.

Detleff smiled contentedly, and ate the rest of his lunch in silence. Apparently he felt that anything after the clean-your-glasses-with-your-fingers trick would have been an anticlimax.

All I have to add about my lunch that day is that Detleff provided the conversational high point.

XVII

By the end of the third day, I hated it. I hated it with all my heart. Nothing was going to change. It was going to be the same, in every class, every day. The only thing I was learning was that boredom can hurt like physical pain, like wearing an iron hat, like sandpaper clothes, like being crushed under a big stone.

I had been told by the other geeks at lunch that there were events from time to time. There would be football games against Riverview's hated rival, Lake View. When those were about to take place, the Riverview students would sing football fight songs in the halls, and all turn up at the park the next day to root and cheer. There would be assemblies, at which Mrs. Costello's public-speaking class would put on patriotic programs. The wheezy Riverview band would give a concert once a year, and we might be shown a twenty-year-old movie around Christmas time.

What I hated more than the stupid notebook system, more than Mrs. Kukla's yelling and Mrs. MacAllister's endless, disgusting Jew phobia, Mr. Moody's whining, and having to see poor Miss Sweet, who belonged in a hospital, every day, was the attitude of the students. They were passive. Nobody complained. With the exception of Linda Pudovkin, who never seemed to be around, I'd met no one who acted as though they didn't like it. Well, that's putting it too strongly—no one acted as though they hated it.

Why didn't people complain? Why weren't they mad? Why didn't they rise up like the proletariat and strike at the bourgeoisie? Instead, everybody marched through the halls like a robot, copied things that meant nothing to them into their notebooks, and sat in the basement and ate their lunches.

By the time 2:15 rolled around and I cut my two study halls and burst out of the building, I was feeling as though I couldn't breathe. I stood on the steps outside the school and gulped air. And that was how I felt after the third full day.

By the end of the third week, I was having thoughts, cruel ones, that made my head feel hot. I wanted to set the place on fire. I wanted to mow people down. When the alligator bit Miss Sweet's finger, I cheered like everybody else. And when Sergeant Gunter read to us, I identified with the *Lumpenproletariat.*

And yet another week dragged past. My uniform arrived.

Before going to bed, I had worked on my uniform. I had removed all the removable insignia and polished them with Brasso and a medium toothbrush. I finished them with a soft thick cloth and then a chamois. They glowed like 24-karat gold, rich and deep and buttery. I cut a slit in a piece of shirt cardboard and slid it behind each button, so I could polish it without getting any Brasso on the fabric, which I had brushed with a whisk broom until it was soft-looking and the brown color had deepened beautifully. Then I replaced the insignia, using a ruler to make sure the round ones, with the R.O.T.C. torch, were the regulation distance from the edges of the lapels, as were the ones in the shape of the letters U.S. The shoes I had polished until they were miraculous.

I hooked the uniform, on its wooden hanger, over the edge of the door, where I could see it first thing when I woke up.

Now it was morning. I was putting on the gleaming thing. The tan cotton shirt, professionally laundered and ironed, the regulation military necktie—I put them on carefully. Then came the United States Army wool serge trousers, size 46, with a knife-edge crease, and the jacket, also size 46. I was transformed into a completely sharp, if round, junior soldier—with bare feet.

Then it was time for my masterstroke. I pulled on the red-and-purple argyle socks. The R.O.T.C. did not supply socks or underwear for cadets. It was the cadet's own responsibility to find black or dark-colored socks to wear with his uniform, and points would be deducted from the cadet's overall score for wearing socks of any other kind. I did not mind that points would be deducted. Not in the least did I mind that points would be deducted.

I'd had a tailor shorten my uniform trousers an extra half inch so my argyles would flash with every step.

I laced my miracle shoes and adjusted my overseas cap, with gleaming, accurately affixed R.O.T.C. badge, at the precise angle, took a last look at myself in the mirror, saluted, and stepped off smartly to begin my fourth Friday—my first Uniform Day—at Riverview High School.

Though I hadn't planned it, this would be the day I would punch Detleff in the stomach. Having thought of me as a fellow geek all these weeks, suddenly seeing me in my shiny R.O.T.C. suit had an unsettling effect on a kid whose family had run away from bullies in uniforms. The punch was just to confirm that nightmares do come true.

I was turning into a horrible person—and the proof of this was that the confused and betrayed look from behind Detleff's greasy glasses did not bother me. On the contrary, I enjoyed it. It was a break in the routine.

XVIII

The next Monday morning was the first morning I did not get off the bus. I didn't plan it. I was feeling typically groggy, sitting all the way in the back. The bus was full of kids on their way to Riverview. It would pull up in front of the school, and everybody would pile out. Then the bus would pull away, and a minute later another one would arrive and disgorge. I just sat in the back, as though I were paralyzed or in some kind of trance. I watched them all get off. I never got up. I never got out.

The doors, front and back, closed with that hissing and thumping noise, and the bus nosed out into traffic. I told myself I would get off at the next stop and walk the two blocks back to the school. I didn't. I didn't get off at the stop after that, either. It was completely easy—I just didn't get off. When I was a few blocks away, the trance lifted, also the dull pain I always felt on the way to school. I can't say I was happy, just not in agony.

I hadn't been happy all weekend. Having punched Detleff in the breadbasket weighed on me. It was not that I hit him hard, and not that he wasn't a boring idiot, and not that other people had not punched him—it was the frame of mind I had been in when I did it. He had made a stupid joke, sniffing into his lunch bag and saying, "My mother made me cheese sandwiches, and how can I tell? The nose knows."

And I hit him. It was not a big deal, really. He acted as though he had forgotten it the next minute, and even repeated his moronic pun to somebody else. But there was that moment when he looked at me. I was finding it hard to get that out of my mind. And Detleff was just the wrong person to hit. My hatred of Riverview had been building for a good while. If I didn't do something antisocial, I felt that I was going to go dead, like the other students. I needed to let out my anger. I needed to hit somebody, but not an insignificant goof from Europe. I needed to hit somebody big. I needed to hit an authority figure. About the only person I had any respect for was Sergeant Gunter—I could have hit him. But he was also the only teacher I liked—and besides, he had killed men in the Pacific and fought Fascism in Spain. I didn't have the kind of nerve it would have taken to hit him.

These thoughts had weighed on me all weekend. I

mostly hung around my room, smoking cigars and listening to the English-language transmission to North America from Radio Moscow on the Hallicrafters.

It had gotten to be October, the leaves were turning brown, and there was a nip in the air. The farther the bus got from the school, the better I felt. I always felt better when I was moving around the streets of Chicago. I had not given up my summertime habit of random wandering. After cutting my two study halls at 2:15, and on weekends, I walked and took buses, and looked at things.

But I had never ridden the bus past Riverview. I had no idea where it went, or where it would wind up. I was the only passenger for a few blocks. Then people started getting on and off, going to work, going shopping.

I rode through the neighborhood, past the low brick buildings with stores on the ground floor and apartments above, old frame houses, and sometimes a small factory, a warehouse, a used-car lot, a cemetery. Then it would start all over again, through another neighborhood, one I didn't know. People got on the bus, people got off.

The bus lurched left onto a diagonal north-south street I'd never seen before. I took notice at once. This was by far the most interesting neighborhood I had seen yet. The houses looked like they might be very old; some of them had sway-backed roofs and leaned toward or away from each other. And some of them had carvings and cutouts and odd decorations on them. Some of them had a sort of fantasy quality, windows of odd shapes, doors covered with sheets of copper, bright colors. I was getting excited. Something about this neighborhood pleased me very much. Maybe it was the size of things—the streets were narrow, and none of the buildings was very large. The stores looked friendly and old-fashioned—lots of them had big potted plants in their windows, and old-timey-looking signs with tarnished gold lettering.

And the people walking around were interesting, too. Some of the men had long hair, and there were women wearing long skirts, bright colors, capes and shawls, and strange-looking jewelry. There were a lot of trees, in big tubs along the sidewalk. I liked this neighborhood.

I had decided to get off the bus and explore on foot for a while. I was just getting out of my seat when I saw something else I wasn't expecting—an ape, a skinny ape hunched over the wheel of an old station wagon. The station wagon careened around a corner and was gone in the couple of seconds it took me to absorb the idea of an ape driving it, run that idea past my brain another time, realize that, of course, it couldn't be an ape, and that it could be, and was, Kenny Papescu.

XIX

Even the sidewalk was not made of the usual sidewalk stuff. It was made of smooth light-brown stone that felt nice underfoot. There was a grocery store with wooden crates of produce outside, under a canvas awning, and some people were picking out their fruit and vegetables, feeling them and sniffing them. There were pots of flowers, too—chrysanthemums. I could smell fresh-baked bread. It had been dim and overcast when the bus pulled away from Riverview High School, but now the sun had come out.

I looked up at the tops of the buildings. They all had interesting shapes, fancy curlicues or geometric patterns, and sometimes a name, *The Fleegle Building*, or a date, *1887*, carved into the brick. The side streets, which connected with the street I was on, had lots of trees and interesting big old houses. Some of the stores had fall leaves and pumpkins and squashes in the windows, with whatever the store sold, shoes or tools or crockery, displayed among the leaves. I imagined that this little neighborhood had not looked any different seventy-five or a hundred years before. I could almost picture the horse-drawn wagons—there were stone blocks next to the curb in front of some of the stores, obviously for people to step on when getting up and down from wagons. There was a stone fountain with a basin facing the street, which had to be for horses to drink from. There was still water pouring into the basin from a spout, which made me wonder if there were still horses around, and then I saw one! It was pulling a wagon full of old broken furniture and junk, driven by an old guy in a beaten-up hat and a shabby coat. It clumped and squeaked and rattled down the street and around a corner.

Everything about this place made me feel sort of warm. It was like a movie set—only it was real.

I saw the old station wagon, parked across the street, at the same moment I heard Kenny Papescu's voice.

"Nifkin! Taking a day off from the House of Pain?"

Kenny Papescu was sitting at one of four or five little tables, arranged on the sidewalk in front of a bakery, drinking a fragrant cup of coffee.

"House of Pain?" I asked him.

"Riverview."

"Oh. Yes."

"Go in and get yourself a coffee, if you like," he said.

"Then come out and join me. I've got a few minutes to kill."

"Thanks. I will," I said.

"They've got some really nice sfogliatelle in there," he said. "I recommend them."

"Sfogliatelle?"

"It's a pastry. They're right on the counter. I could stand another one myself. Here's thirty-five cents."

I refused his money. "My treat," I said.

"Thanks," Kenny Papescu said.

I went into the bakery, which smelled wonderfully. A fat lady fixed me a coffee and handed me two sfogliatelle, on sheets of waxed paper, which I carried outside.

The pastry was crunchy and chewy and flaky, and had something unidentifiable and delicious in it. The coffee was creamy and hot and strong. I sat at the little table with Kenny Papescu, getting crumbs on myself and feeling content.

"If you're not doing anything, you can help me deliver something," Kenny said. "There's five bucks in it for you."

"Sure," I said. "I have nothing special to do."

"Just cutting school, huh?"

"Yes."

"I did that once, a couple of years ago," Kenny Papescu said.

"What did they say about it?" I asked.

"I don't know," Kenny Papescu said. "I haven't been back to find out."

I assumed Kenny was kidding. It wasn't possible, I thought, to cut school for two years without anybody doing anything about it. On the other hand, Kenny Papescu did seem to come and go as he pleased—as did his girlfriend, Linda Pudovkin, who I had only seen a couple of times since the beginning of school. I experienced a moment of worry about what would happen to me when I went back to Riverview, and then shook it off.

"What are we delivering?" I asked.

"*La Mesa de los Pecados Capitales,*" Kenny said.

"Huh?"

"*The Table of the Seven Deadly Sins.* It's a work of art, painted by Hieronymus Bosch in the fifteenth century. It's a table with a picture on top. We're taking it to a rich guy in the suburbs."

"Wow. Is it an original?"

"So my dad says. There's one in the Prado museum in Spain, but it's probably a fake. This one's genuine. My dad put six coats of bowling-alley polyurethane on it so glasses won't leave a ring."

"Is this true?" I asked Kenny Papescu.

"Nah, we copied it from a book. I did some of the painting myself. But don't say anything in case the guy wants to believe it's real."

"Ah, so this one is the fake."

"Nope. This is the real one, painted by Bosch himself."

"You just said it was fake."

"It is."

"Which is it, fake or real?"

Kenny gave me a broad smile. "Take your pick."

"Ah, I get it . . . sort of . . . I think."

XX

Kenny told me the guy we were going to deliver the table to was Miles Greenthorpe. Miles was famous. He was on television every night, selling discount major home appliances—stoves, freezers, washing machines. He sponsored the late movie on Channel 7. Miles was famous for jumping around and waving his arms and yelling and getting spit on the camera lens.

"He's a celebrity," Kenny said. "There's no way on earth he's going to tip us less than fifty."

"Really?"

"He tips me fifty once in a while, when I drive Pamela home from school."

"Who's Pamela?"

"His daughter."

"You know her, huh?"

"You looking for a girlfriend?" Kenny asked.

"Not exactly," I said.

"Well, Pamela is looking for a boyfriend," Kenny said.

"She is?"

"She is."

We motored along. I gazed out the windows. The suburbs are clean and open, the streets are wide, and there are lots of junk-food places.

"So, Pamela goes to Riverview?" I asked.

"No, she doesn't."

"Oh. I thought you knew her from school."

"I do. From the Wheaton School. I don't go to Riverview. Officially, I go to Wheaton. Officially."

"Oh, I see," I said.

"No, you don't," said Kenny Papescu.

Miles Greenthorpe's house had two concrete lions, bigger than life-size, flanking the entrance to the driveway. The house was very large, made of rough white marble blocks, with green shutters on the windows, Greek columns, and a couple of pointy towers with shingled roofs and gold eagles on top.

"Miles designed the house himself," Kenny said.

"It's real unusual," I said. "My parents would like to see it."

My parents would not only have liked to see the interior of Miles Greenthorpe's house, they would possibly have died of pure joy at the way it was decorated. There was a lot of stuff spray-painted gold, realistic plastic house plants, and white carpets so thick you wobbled when you walked. There were a lot of new-looking antiques and works of art.

Miles Greenthorpe was a little guy with a red mustache.

"Bring it right in, boys," Miles Greenthorpe said. "Let's have a look at it."

I helped Kenny unwrap the table.

"It looks great," Miles Greenthorpe said. "Did you bring the document?"

"Oh, yeh, the authentication," Kenny said. "Got it right here."

Kenny pulled a rolled-up paper from his back pocket and read aloud:

"Painted by Hieronymous or Jerome Bosch, born around 1450, died 1516, who spent his entire artistic career in the small Dutch town of Hertogenbosch, from which he derived his name. He was an eccentric painter of religious visions, specializing in the torments of hell. His work was favored by the noble families of the Netherlands, Austria, and Spain.

"*The Table of the Seven Deadly Sins* consists of four small circles surrounding a larger one that is divided into scenes depicting the seven capital sins, Anger, Pride, Lust, Sloth, Gluttony, Avarice, and Envy.

"This work belonged to Philip II of Spain and was kept at El Escorial. It was transferred to the Prado during the Spanish Civil War, for safety. At some point, it was secretly sold to Samuel Klugarsh, the famous collector, and a fiendishly clever copy was substituted in its place.

"During World War II, Klugarsh smuggled some of the major pieces in his collection to South America, and the table was probably among them. The collection dropped out of sight for several years, and the table resurfaced in the possession of Wallace Nussbaum, a colonel in the Chilean Army. Nussbaum fell afoul of the law while in the United States and was sentenced to Devil's Island for minting his own stamps. His possessions were seized by the U.S. Postal Service and sold at one of the regular auctions, held twice a year, to dispose of unclaimed and impounded goods. The bulk of Nussbaum's lot consisted of statuary depicting chickens and was of no particular value. The table was not recognized as an important work of art by the postal authorities, and the lot was bid on and acquired by Anton Papescu of Chicago."

"See, it's signed by Kevin Shapiro, Professor of Art History at Miskatonic University," Kenny said, pointing to the signature at the bottom.

Miles Greenthorpe took the scroll from Kenny and examined it.

"This seems to be in order," Miles Greenthorpe said.

XXI

"Your father did a great job on the restoration," Miles Greenthorpe said.

"That's moisture-cure polyurethane," Kenny said. "It's what they use on bowling alleys. Treat it as rough as you like."

"You're a good boy," Miles Greenthorpe said. "Is this your friend?"

"Permit me to introduce Robert Nifkin, my assistant," Kenny said. "My unsalaried assistant."

Miles Greenthorpe fished two hundred-dollar bills out of his pocket and tucked them into our shirt pockets, one with each hand.

"Come with me, boys," he said. "I want to show you something that will make better Americans of you."

We followed Miles Greenthorpe down a hallway and into a huge room with little wooden Cupids hanging from the ceiling, chandeliers, paintings, and gold-

pickled furniture that would have caused my parents to lose control.

"The master bedroom," Miles Greenthorpe said. "And now, kindly step this way."

We were in a bathroom, a little bigger than my bedroom at home.

"Kindly note that I am not touching any switches," Miles Greenthorpe said. The bathroom had been dark when we entered, but as soon as we were through the door, a dim pink light, like early dawn, had slowly come up.

"Now watch what happens as I approach the commode," Miles Greenthorpe said. The toilet was suddenly bathed in soft green light.

"All done with electric eyes. Green, when the seat is down," Miles Greenthorpe said. "Now observe."

Miles lifted the seat, and the green light extinguished. In its place a red light came on and cast a round circle on the surface of the water. Miles unzipped his pants and peed into the toilet.

"You see," he said, while peeing, "should my wife awaken in the night, needing to use the facilities, the green light tells her the seat is safely down. Thus, uncomfortable errors while half-asleep are avoided. Conversely, I, without need of fully illuminating the bathroom, am provided with a useful target."

Miles passed a hand over the toilet, without touching it. It flushed. Zipping his fly, he asked, "If either of you would have need?"

We mumbled no thanks.

"Of course, we have a bidet, also electronic," Miles Greenthorpe said. "Here is the three-way full-length mirror, the sunlamps are recessed in the ceiling, and step on this scale, Robert."

I stepped on the scale. A smooth-sounding female recorded voice said, "Two hundred and twenty-two pounds."

"I bet you're a football player," Miles Greenthorpe said. "Now I call your attention to the shower. Eight high-pressure nozzles at different heights and angles, and the hi-fi speakers are waterproof."

He turned on the shower, tiny spotlights came on, and opera sounded from the speakers.

"All Italian marble, of course," he said. "The towel rack is electrically heated, so you dry with a toasty towel, and this is a nice accessory—just step onto this platform."

I stepped. It was a vibrating foot massager.

"Now, boys, when I was your age, we were poor. We lived in the tenements. The toilet was in a little closet in the public hallway. We shared it with four other families. The bathtub was in the kitchen. And some people lived in places where there were still outhouses in the back yard.

"In only thirty years I have come from that . . . to this. And that is why I show you this magnificent bathroom. This is the true meaning of life in our great democracy. Any one of us, through hard work and dedication, can achieve a bathroom like this, and all that it stands for. I hope you will remember that."

We told Miles Greenthorpe that we'd never forget it.

He was a nice guy, and proud of his bathroom. None of us could know, of course, standing there in the pink light, that he would die in that bathroom a year later, electrocuted in a freak household accident. In a way, he would give his life for capitalism.

"Are you heading downtown?" Miles Greenthorpe asked. "Maybe you could give Pamela a ride. She has an appointment at the orthodontist's."

XXII

Pamela Greenthorpe's face, lips, and eyebrows were covered with pale, almost white, makeup. She was dressed entirely in black. She had descended the staircase with the gilded handrail in Miles Greenthorpe's house, pausing on each step. Then she glided toward us, silently.

"Kenny is going to give you a ride downtown, honey," Miles Greenthorpe said. "And this is Kenny's friend Robert."

"Kenny. Robert."

Pamela spoke our names in a tone of voice such that she might have been saying "Doom" or "All is lost" or "We are all damned." Not "Oh no! We are all damned!" but "We are all damned, and there is nothing to be done about it." Sort of a depressed exhaling voice.

She looked like she was going to a funeral. She

sounded like she was going to a funeral. When she got in the car, I felt like we were going to a funeral.

Pamela sat in the back seat, behind me. Kenny gunned the engine. He had a little smile playing over his face.

I tried to make conversation. "Did you see the table we delivered? Your father was really pleased with it."

"My father is a boor," Pamela said. "He has tiny tree frogs on his soul. Did he show you his bathroom?"

"Yes," I said.

"Pathetic," Pamela breathed.

"I thought the talking scale was kind of neat," I said.

Pamela covered her face with her hands and gave a blood-chilling scream. "I can't stand it!" she wailed.

Then she sat, perfectly composed, gazing straight ahead.

"Pamela has *Weltschmerz*," Kenny said.

"She does?"

"Yes," Kenny said. "Pamela's got *Weltschmerz*, and she's got it bad. Isn't that so, Pamela?"

"My name is Nastasia," Pamela breathed.

Kenny was trying to suppress a smile. I couldn't tell if they were both putting me on, or just him.

"Nastasia? I thought it was Pamela," I said.

"*Weltschmerz*," Pamela/Nastasia said.

"What's *Weltschmerz*?" I asked.

"My heart is an empty cat-food can, rusty, smelly, the jagged edges cut my flesh."

"Oh," I said.

"Damn right," Kenny said.

We motored along.

"Been to school lately, Nastasia?" Kenny asked.

"I drop in from time to time," Nastasia said. "It's more or less as you remember it. They ask about you."

"Give them my love," Kenny said.

Nastasia poked the back of my head with a finger.

"Who's he?" she asked.

"Robert? Robert goes to Riverview. Linda met him. She says he's the only interesting person there."

This came as a surprise to me. I had only ever talked to Linda twice.

"Robert, your head is a nice shape," Nastasia said. "It's round."

"I pride myself on the roundness of my head," I said.

"The rest of you is round, too," Nastasia said.

"I pride myself on that, too," I said.

"He's a well-rounded person," Kenny said.

"Ohh! A Volkswagen!" Nastasia said. "They look to me like little unborn antelopes. So sweet."

I was getting the hang of conversation with Nastasia.

"Would either of you care for a cigar?" I asked.

Nastasia's slightly pudgy hand shot over the seat-back, next to my head.

"Gimme," she said.

I handed back a Wolf Brothers Rum-Soaked Crook.

97

Nastasia leaned over the seat, and I lit it for her, and lit one for myself. Kenny declined to smoke.

"This is good. It tastes like squirrels at play," Nastasia said.

"To me, they taste like an empty gymnasium in the moonlight," I said.

Nastasia held her cigar between her fingers and blew a smoke ring. "Yes, you're right," she said.

Kenny brought the car to a stop.

"Here we are," he said.

Nastasia leaned over the seat, snapped my head back, and kissed me. The lit end of the cigar in her left hand was close enough to my cheek for me to feel the heat. The combination of being surprised, being kissed, and being scared I was about to be branded with a Wolf Brothers Rum-Soaked Crook made for a unique sensation.

Then Nastasia, puffing her stogie, got out of the car and headed for a familiar-looking luncheonette.

"Isn't that . . . ?"

"Dr. Pudovkin's office," Kenny said.

"I thought the orthodontist."

"Nah. Miles says that. He's embarrassed she goes to a shrink."

"What's wrong with her besides the obvious?" I asked.

"Nothing," Kenny said. "Nastasia is a cool girl. She seemed to take to you right off. Not many she likes."

"So, I should feel honored?"

"Well, be careful. If she liked you a whole lot, she would probably have shoved the cigar up your nose."

"Complicated girl, huh?"

"Exactly."

XXIII

The feeling of hatred and despair didn't become over-whelming until the bus pulled up outside Riverview. This was not the day following my cutting school, meeting Kenny Papescu, delivering the table to Miles Greenthorpe, and being kissed by his daughter Pamela, who called herself Nastasia. It was the day after that.

Actually, nothing had happened when I walked into school after being away for a whole day without an excuse. Nobody said anything. Nobody noticed. No-body cared. Of course! Why hadn't I known that? It could have been the motto of the school. They could have carved it over the door: *We Don't Care.*

Mrs. Kukla bellowed at us as usual. The kids shuffled their feet or slumped in their seats. The usual foul odors wafted through the halls. It was another bone-crushing, mind-killing day at Riverview . . . and yet, there was a note of tension.

Mrs. Kukla's standard warning against Communists was shouted a little louder: "Students, I hope you will remember that Mrs. Kukla has been telling you that the Reds are everywhere, looking to influence the boy, or be it a girl, which are not vigilant. Those Commies could be your best friend. You never know. So Beware! And if someone starts in to indoctrinate, just put your finger in your ears and say the Pledge of Allegiance or otherwise the Lord's Prayer, whichever is applicable."

In the hall, right after homeroom was over, who should sidle up to me in the hall but my recent victim, Detleff.

"Be careful," Detleff whispered. "They're watching you."

"What are you talking about, idiot-from-Europe?" I asked. I was over being scared I would get in trouble for cutting school, and was already in my half-asleep mode.

"*Staatspolizei,*" Defleff hissed. "Guys in raincoats. They watch people like you."

Detleff's face was sweaty and he looked truly scared . . . or crazy. I assumed the latter.

"Listen, I'm sorry, but I can't afford to be seen talking to you," Detleff said. "Better pretend you don't know me, okay?"

"I *don't* know you," I said. "At least, I don't want to."

Detleff patted my shoulder. "Thanks," he said. "And good luck. Just stay away from the R.O.T.C. room."

Then he faded into the mass of students swarming through the halls.

This encounter with Detleff was mildly interesting. I'd never thought of him as having enough brains to be mentally ill. Of course, it could have been his feeble idea of some kind of revenge for my having punched him in the tummy. He might have been trying to make me paranoid—but was he a good-enough actor? He had looked really frightened.

It didn't take ten seconds for me to decide to forget all about Detleff's weird behavior. But then I saw Lance Lashway, and Lance was looking as odd as Detleff, not scared like Detleff, but definitely excited.

"You missed it," Lance said. "It happened right outside the school. Right on the sidewalk."

"What happened?" I asked him. The look on his face led me to suspect there had been a murder, or some other interesting spectacle, and naturally it had to be on the one day I decided to cut school.

"They arrested him," Lance said. "It was just like the movies. Two guys, federal agents. They collared him, drove him away in a gray Plymouth."

I was almost following this. Detleff's warning had something to do with it. I felt queasy.

"Who? Who got arrested?"

"Sergeant Gunter," Lance said. "He's a subversive."

"He's a homo?"

"No, he's un-American," Lance said. "Not pervert . . . subvert. He's been subverting us."

"This is one of those rumors that go around schools," I said. "Like the one about how FanTan chewing gum contains opium."

"I didn't know that," Lance said. "They sell it all over."

"Or that if you put aspirins in a girl's Coke, she will have sex with you."

"So? What's your point?" Lance Lashway asked.

"My point is, he probably wasn't arrested. Maybe his mother is sick or his house caught fire or something. It's just a rumor."

"No, people saw it," Lance said.

"What people?" I asked.

"I don't know. People," Lance said.

"Yeh. Right. I'll bet Sergeant Gunter is in the R.O.T.C. room when we get there, same as always."

"Sergeant Gunter is in the federal clink, where he belongs," Lance said. "He was trying to un-Americanize us."

In the R.O.T.C. room, when we got there, was Principal Fruhling and a guy in a gray suit.

"Little snotnose sissies!" Helmet Fruhling roared. "Every teacher in this school is instructed to tell you over and over that you are supposed to report anyone who tries to indoctrinate you or hand you propaganda.

Not one of you too-feeble-to-take-gym babies came to my office or anywhere else to tell us that bum Gunter was reading to you right out of Karl for-Christ's-sake Marx!

"This is Agent Pomeroy. He is going to be here for the next few days, interviewing you Tovariches one by one. Cooperate fully. After he's done, I am closing down this Commie cell, and you fairies will all take Remedial Phys. Ed."

Every time I had seen Principal Fruhling he was red-faced and in a rage; now he was purple, and spitting when he spoke. So Riverview *did* care—about some things.

I caught a glimpse of Lance Lashway. He was standing at attention, his jaw set, his head high, gazing nobly through his glasses. All at once I knew he was the one. He had blown the whistle on Sergeant Gunter.

XXIV

That was the day before. Now, as the bus pulled up, I thought I could already smell the fartlike aroma of the cafeteria. I felt my guts spasm, and I knew I wasn't going in.

Agent Pomeroy was not going to get any cooperation from me.

I had Kenny Papescu's phone number in my wallet. I thought I might call him and see if he needed any help. First, I was going to find out the address of the federal clink and send Sergeant Gunter a box of fifty Wolf Brothers Rum-Soaked Crooks.

XXV

Weeks passed.

Chicago winters are fierce. I once heard an old sourdough interviewed on the radio who said that he had come nearer dying of exposure in Chicago than he ever had in the Klondike. It seems he had gotten frosted lungs on Michigan Avenue when he walked a block from his hotel to buy a newspaper.

As the weather got colder I would sometimes drop in at Riverview, just to get some shelter. Also, it was fascinating to notice that it was hardly ever mentioned that I was in attendance not one day in five, and when it was, the school was powerless to do anything about it. I was making a bit of money helping Kenny with occasional deliveries. We had become friends. Now and then I'd meet Kenny and Linda at Mel's for an infusion of hot grease.

The rest of the time, I continued urban hiking and exploring. I spent a fair amount of time in the reading room of the main library, specializing in American poets and novels, and there was the good old Clark Theater, fifty cents at all times if you had a college I.D. card. I had one. Kenny had helped me fix it up. I was Noel Swerdlow, nineteen years old, and a student at the University of Chicago. It had my picture and a current date—Swerdlow had attended in the late 1940s. Since I was sharing his identity, I represented Noel by attending lectures at the university. The card got me in. My favorites were in the area of Art History, especially ones about architecture.

I thought I was free, but the system was toying with me. I could have been snatched at any moment. My time was coming, though I knew it not. I had spent a pleasant fifteen minutes with Mr. Gerrold, the school psychologist, German teacher, and glee-club director. It was a routine interview. Everybody got one once in four years. When I mentioned that I was hardly ever there, he delved into why I cut school. He failed to find a deeper reason than that I hated it there.

He was a likable man, and popular with everyone, though he readily admitted that his background was not in psych. This made no difference, as his recommendations were ignored by everyone. So I thought.

More to the point was Mr. Finger, the school

attendance officer, to whose office I was sent now and then. Mr. Finger assigned me to various disciplinary activities, detention after school, a special homeroom for incorrigibles, and a motivational gym class—none of which punishments I ever turned up for, as they tended to take place during school hours, and as I have said, I was seldom available.

Letters to my parents were entrusted to me for delivery. I simply neglected to deliver them, or typed letters to Mr. Finger, over a facsimile of my father's signature.

The first my father would know about my months of truancy would be when he got a registered letter from the Board of Education telling him that my transfer to Anton Mesmer High School—a holding pen for delinquents on their way to careers in professional crime—was scheduled for the following week. If I failed to show up, a Cook County deputy sheriff would be paying a call with a court summons. Mr. Finger's and Mr. Gerrold's reports had finally been read at the main office, and Mr. Finger had told me the letter was already working its way through the bowels of the bureaucracy.

Slashings and beatings were said to be daily occurrences at Mesmer. The boys who went there were drooling, mouth-breathing throwbacks without foreheads, and the teachers were sadists, defrocked correction officers, and former students. Truants and incorrigibles who continued to resist were given into the hands of social workers, by whom they were then destroyed.

My ass, as Mr. Finger was fond of saying, was grass.

XXVI

It was important to me that I not be transferred to Mesmer. I had to make a plausible argument as to why my father should rescue me from being sent to such a place, and come up with a reasonable alternative. I had an alternative in mind.

One night, when we were driving around, Kenny had asked me if I wanted to see his school. We drove to a fancy residential neighborhood—the Gold Coast. Kenny pulled up in front of a darkened old mansion. The garden behind the high iron fence was overgrown, and the place appeared deserted.

"We can get in around the side," Kenny said.

"This is a school? We're going in?" I was a little apprehensive. Kenny was fairly wild. It wouldn't have been totally out of character for him to get me involved in housebreaking.

"It's a private school. I come here all the time. We'll visit one of the teachers."

"What would a teacher be doing here at this time of night?"

"He lives upstairs—in the servants' quarters. It's all right. Come on."

Kenny led me around the side of the building. Off a cobblestone alley, he pushed open a black metal door—a service entrance. We entered a dimly lit corridor.

We passed a row of trash cans, and through a door into a huge kitchen.

"You hungry?" Kenny asked. He was rummaging in a large refrigerator. On a worktable he plunked an industrial-size bologna, a half onion, a tomato. Then he went to a cupboard and withdrew a large rye bread. He slid open a drawer and removed a knife. In a minute, Kenny had carved massive slices. He handed me a sandwich four inches thick.

"Take this with you," he said. "We'll go upstairs and see Wally Gershkowitz."

Now, sandwich in hand, I followed Kenny up a steep flight of stairs. I had never been in a house like this, but I got the idea that this was a back stairway for the use of servants. We climbed four steep flights and emerged in a narrow hallway with doors on both sides.

"This is where the maids and such used to sleep," Kenny said. "Now just Gershkowitz lives up here, and a couple old ladies—aunts of the headmistress, I think. Here—knock on this door."

I knocked. As I did so, Kenny somehow faded away completely. He must have backed suddenly into one of the other rooms. I became aware of his absence at the same moment that the door opened and I found myself holding the enormous sandwich, looking into a tiny room, and being looked at through a haze of cigarette smoke by three people.

Wally Gershkowitz was easily the ugliest person I had ever seen. In his late twenties, he was swarthy, unshaven, and short, with a shock of coarse black hair, pale brown eyes, a pig's snout, and a sneering expression. He held a Lucky Strike cigarette between the yellowed second and third fingers of his left hand. I liked him immediately.

In the room with Gershkowitz were two kids my age. One was Pamela/Nastasia Greenthorpe. As usual, her lips and eyebrows were covered with almost-white makeup. She was dressed entirely in black. The boy was wearing a cheap-looking suit, a ghastly necktie, and had pointed black shoes out of all proportion to his height, which was under five feet. His spotty face resembled that of some kind of rodent.

I was looking around for Papescu.

"Who are you?" Gershkowitz bellowed. I felt like an idiot.

"I'm an idiot," I said.

"Good!" Gershkowitz shouted. "Only idiots allowed here! Come in!"

"This is Nastasia Greenthorpe," Gershkowitz said, indicating the girl. "Nastasia, this is an idiot." Nastasia smiled a sickly, bitter smile.

"We've met."

"And this is Clifton Fadiman," Gershkowitz said. "No relation."

Clifton snickered and hunched his shoulders up and down. "Hey, an idiot! An idiot!" he said, giving a pretty good imitation of one.

"And what brings you to my door, idiot?" Gershkowitz thundered.

"Kenny Papescu brings me to your door," I said.

"Papescu! Papescu here? He'd better not show his face!" Gershkowitz roared. "I've told him I want my Boy Scout ax returned. If I don't get it, he is going to be a very sorry Papescu!"

"Does anybody want this sandwich?" I asked, feeling uncomfortable.

"I want it!" Clifton Fadiman said.

"Give!" Gershkowitz growled. He took the sandwich, tore off about a third for Fadiman, and attacked the rest. "You want?" he asked Nastasia, gesturing with the ragged hunk of sandwich. She shook her head slowly and smiled her rueful smile.

Kenny came in, eating his sandwich.

"Papescu!" Gershkowitz threatened.

"I forgot it again. It's leaning against the wall, next to the door of my room. I'll bring it, I promise."

"You'd better, Papescu. I'm losing patience with you." Gershkowitz glowered.

"Wally is my Science teacher," Kenny said.

"Some student," Gershkowitz muttered.

"What kind of school is this?" I asked.

XXVII

"It isn't a school, it's fantasy land," Gershkowitz said.

"It's a neat school," Nastasia said in her thrilling monotone. "You can do whatever you like."

"I haven't been to a class in six weeks," Clifton Fadiman said. "I've been shooting craps in the basement with some of the kitchen help."

"It's a garbage can," Gershkowitz said.

"My Social Studies teacher is a disciple of Gandhi and Meher Baba," Nastasia said. "He was teaching us about nonviolence, and then he took a vow of silence. Now we just sit and contemplate for one hour every day."

"That is Mr. Fish. He's a fruitcake," Gershkowitz said.

"I think he's spiritual," Nastasia said.

"It was no great loss when he renounced the intellect in favor of spinning, chanting, and rhythmic breathing," Gershkowitz said.

"No, he's a real intellectual," Nastasia said. "He went to Harvard and everything."

An idea was forming. "Who do you have to be to go here?" I asked.

"I think they limit enrollment to humans—for the most part," Gershkowitz said, "unless you pay in advance."

"And you can sort of—do whatever you want?"

"That's not the policy—just the reality. It is not what you would call a tight ship. Right, Papescu?"

"Wally is making fun of me because I'm graduating this year," Kenny said.

"But you don't go to school," I said.

"They don't know that," Kenny said.

XXVIII

"Dad, I want to talk to you about changing schools."

"Yeh, little bestid. I expected."

"Well, Riverview doesn't offer many academic advantages."

"How would you know? You heffent been dere in months already."

How did he know that? I had intercepted every letter from the authorities.

I figured it was a bluff, and I ignored it. "You know, only five or six kids out of a graduating class of three hundred go on to college."

"Is det so? How many go to collitch from deh reformatory, bum?"

The old son-of-a-bitch was omniscient. As usual, he had either found out or guessed all the facts.

I pressed on. "I'm getting serious about my education."

"You mean you're serious det dose Polish boyez on deh Vest Side vill kick your fet tuchas into deh mittle of next veek, yes?" He was enjoying himself. "Listen, in Varshava, mein brudders and I vould make shit out of deh odder gengsters. Maybe I let you go to Mesmer, you should learn how to put up your dukes, little sissyboy."

"Dad, this is America! You had seven brothers. If they send me there, I'll be all alone. Besides, you got kicked out of Warsaw. I'm just getting kicked out of a high school!"

"Yeh, but it vas deh Jews det kicked me out. Deh gentiles vas afraid to touch me."

This, as far as family tradition went, was true. My father had been invited to leave Warsaw by a deputation of Jews belonging to decent middle-class families. They bought him his fare and took him in person to the railroad station. He did well in his adopted country and married a number of women—more or less at the same time—and settled finally with one of them, Faye, my mother, who now spoke: "Philip, don't send him to that place. It's full of Communists and fairies. I have always wanted my son to go to a prep school."

"I'll send him in the navy," Philip said. "Let him play hooky off a ship, the little lowlife." My father had enjoyed *Billy Budd* in a Yiddish translation. His opinion was that Billy got what was coming to him. The idea of 'prenticing me out before the mast always amused him,

118

and it was a sign that he probably didn't have any dia-
bolical plans for me at the moment.

"Hokay, he can go to school vit cepitalists and fairies
instead." He gave me a blow to the head—but not a
hard one. My ass was saved.

XXIX

The Wheaton School was the property of two old sisters. Miss Josephine was the headmistress, and actually owned the building, once the home of the richest family in Chicago. Miss Jean—who was the only woman I have ever seen wearing pince-nez eyeglasses, with a black ribbon attached to them yet—was the principal. They were both lifelong professional educators, and Jean had been a missionary to the Navajos.

I liked Miss Jean, and did not like Miss Josephine. This turned out to be the general opinion. Both of them appeared to be deep in self-delusion, but the popular suspicion was that Josephine was faking it. They were both fat, white-haired women, and they both wore flouncy black dresses.

The building was actually beautiful. The rooms, somewhat the worse for wear, were large and elegant.

There was a spacious entrance hall, a spiral staircase rising from it, which had been somebody's masterpiece. When my mother and I came for my application/entrance interview/acceptance to the Wheaton School, the first thing we saw was a body falling from an upper floor, down through the repeated oval of that staircase, and thudding to the marble floor. This was followed by a cheer.

Miss Jean appeared in the same moment. "Those boys!" she dithered. "They've been dropping that mannequin from the third floor all day. What must you think of such morbid goings-on, Mrs. Nifkin. Do come and meet my sister, Josephine."

The fattest man I had ever seen in my life popped through a doorway and shouted up the staircase—with a lisp, "Enough of this Grand Guignol, Mr. Richard Peterkin! I've had all I can stand of falling bodies, do you hear? I shall expire!" A five-hundred-pound sissy. He dabbed at his forehead with a handkerchief and waddled off, stage right.

"Mr. Saunders, our Drama and Home Economics teacher," Miss Jean said. "The pupils love him."

Throughout, Miss Jean was flouncing around, herding us into an open doorway like a Shetland sheepdog. A little bald-headed man in a shabby suit was coming out.

"This is my colleague Mr. Baker," Miss Jean said. "He

is the principal of the lower school and History teacher in the high school. Mr. Baker, Mrs. Nifkin—and her son."

Mr. Baker produced a long note, inhuman-sounding, like a dial tone. "Ehhhhhhh. I am pleased to meet you. Is this young man to join us?" His dentures clicked.

"Yes, Mr. Baker."

"Ehhhhhhh. Student or faculty?"

"Young Mr. Nifkin will be a student in the high school," Miss Jean said patiently.

"Ehhhhhhh. Capital. Capital. He will be in my class, no doubt."

"We are going to discuss his program presently, Mr. Baker."

"She's a wonderful woman," he said to my mother, and ran up the staircase.

I observed what I took to be Wheaton students drifting in and out of the lobby. They were a mixed bag. Some of them looked exactly like the photos in the school brochure, a copy of which I had brought home to aid in persuading my father. They were dressed in sweaters, white shoes, neat hair, carrying stacks of books. Others were dressed and slouched in the manner of street toughs: leather jackets, engineer boots, black jeans. I saw a couple of girls turned out in a sluttish manner, with net stockings, thick makeup, outlandish hairdos. No one seemed to be going anywhere in a hurry. Kids wandered in and out of the building.

On the front steps, they smoked cigarettes. It was mid-morning. Presumably, somewhere in the building, classes were going on. Nobody seemed to give a damn. It was lovely.

Miss Jean finally shooed us into Miss Josephine's office, which was large and light. Miss Josephine, sitting at a large, messy desk, greeted us distractedly and launched into a discussion of fees with my mother. A check was written, and Miss Josephine suggested that my mother leave me to simply "wander around" for the rest of the day.

"We'll have tested him and worked out his program in a day or two," she said. "Meanwhile, Robert might like to just spend some time looking at our school, talking to the other students, and getting used to us."

XXX

My mother left. I stood in the entry hall. I wasn't quite sure where to go. Clifton Fadiman entered, exhaling his last drag. "Hey, the idiot! You enrolled?"

"Yeh. I guess I am."

"Well, don't stand around here in the lobby, man. Miss Jean will grab you and get you to move furniture or something. Come on and meet everybody."

Clifton took my arm and made to lead me out the front door.

"Where are we going?"

"Out."

"You just came in."

"I just came in to see if anything was happening. Nothing is. I'll take you to the Busy Bun—the whole school's there at one time or another."

The Busy Bun was a luncheonette on the corner of Clark Street and North Avenue. It was long and narrow. A counter ran the length of the place, and there were maybe twenty booths opposite. Most of them were full of kids. Some of them I recognized from the lobby of the Wheaton School. Wally Gershkowitz and Nastasia were sitting in one of the booths, making clouds of smoke. Clifton and I joined them.

"So you joined up, eh?" Gershkowitz asked.

"Just now," I said.

"I believe that, like in the Foreign Legion, it would be bad form to ask you what crimes you committed on the outside—but I will ask you one question, if you have no objection."

"None."

"My question is this: Are you still educable, or are you just another fuck-up?"

"Am I what?"

"The question was plainly stated. Is there any chance that you possess a salvageable brain, or have your parents just parked you here because they know or sense that you can't get kicked out of Wheaton? In other words, is there a glimmer of light upstairs, or are you just a fuck-up?"

"I'm not sure."

"Acceptable answer. You may continue to sit with us."

"Thank you."

"And you may buy Cokes for us."

"My pleasure."

"Nastasia, do you approve of this young man?"

Nastasia had not said a word as yet, or acknowledged me. "I have loved him from the first moment I saw him," she said. This made my head swim.

"Therefore, I can have nothing to do with him, ever." It swam some more.

"Nastasia is a complicated girl," Gershkowitz said. "You may come to appreciate her in time."

"Or not," Clifton Fadiman put in.

"Or not," said Gershkowitz.

"Why is everybody hanging around here?" I asked, wishing to change the subject. I felt Nastasia's eyes not looking at me.

"Many people find Wheaton hard to take early in the day, so they shelter here for a few hours. The Busy Bun has execrable food and would not survive without us. It's as good a place as any, for our purposes."

"Which are?"

"One of them is to drink Coca-Cola, if you would be so kind."

"Of course," I said. I ordered four Cokes from John, the sweating, hairy, beady-eyed proprietor. John was in the act of handing me the Cokes when he spied someone coming in the door.

"Hey! You get outs of here, dzerk-off! Bead it!" A tall, confused-looking man in a tweed jacket stood in the doorway.

"Mr. Koutris, I . . . I . . ."

"You get outs, masturbator!" John shouted. "Or I call Miss Josephine and she comes and trow you outs!"

The man in the tweed stammered a bit more and gesticulated meaninglessly.

John glared at him.

He left.

Clifton Fadiman took all this in with acute pleasure.

"That is Mr. Clarence Fish," he chortled. "He tries to get in here about once a week, and John chases him out."

"Who is he?" I asked.

"He's a teacher. Apparently, his vow of silence doesn't apply to ordering in restaurants. A couple of months ago he had a difference of opinion with John. Fish orders toast. John is rinsing out a few dishes at the time and handles the toast with soapy fingers. Fish complains that he wants other toast. John asks why. Fish says that John has handled the toast with dirty fingers. This offends John. He argues that his hands couldn't be cleaner, having just come from soap and water. Fish insists. John bans Fish from the place. Fish wants to discuss it, but John is still mad."

"Poor Clarence," Nastasia said. "I have to go comfort him." She dashed out of the Busy Bun.

XXXI

"Hey! Here's the man himself!" Clifton Fadiman shouted. A handsome boy in a very nice sport jacket had approached the booth. "This is Jeremy Holtz," Clifton said, "the best kid in the whole school."

Jeremy Holtz beamed. He shook my hand firmly. "I'm pleased to make your acquaintance." He smiled. He had very white, regular teeth.

"Join us, Jeremy," Gershkowitz said. It was the first time I had seen him smile.

"I can only stay a little while," Jeremy Holtz said. "I have to go and help Mr. Matanuska shovel snow." He consulted a beautiful gold watch. "I'll stay five minutes, okay? Would you permit me to buy you all sweet rolls—or anything you like?"

"Thanks, Jeremy," Clifton said. "I'll have one. Wally? Robert?"

"Nothing for me, thanks," Gershkowitz said.

"Maybe you would like a steak, Mr. Gershkowitz," Jeremy said. "Or an order of fried chicken. I could give you five dollars if you need some money."

"Nothing for me, Jeremy," Gershkowitz said.

"Mr. Koutris, three sweet rolls for my friends, please," Jeremy called.

"Rights away, Mr. Holtz." John smiled. He instantly brought the sweet rolls to the booth. "I bring you four coffees, on the house, my friends," he said, stroking Jeremy's hair.

"I noticed you looking at my watch," Jeremy said to me. "If you like, I can give it to you."

Gershkowitz shook his head.

"That's very kind, Jeremy, but I couldn't accept it."

"Why?" Jeremy asked, looking a little hurt.

"I have a watch," I said. "You keep yours."

"Okay," Jeremy said. "I'm going to shovel snow pretty soon." He sipped his coffee. He looked at his watch again.

"Sure you wouldn't like to have this, Robert? It's a Rolex."

"No, really. Thanks just the same."

"Well, I'd better be going or Mr. Matanuska will start without me." Jeremy Holtz shook my hand. "I hope you enjoy going to Wheaton, Robert. It's the best school in the world."

"Thanks, Jeremy."

Jeremy left the Busy Bun, waving and shaking hands with everybody in the place.

"What's with him?" I asked.

"He's the nicest kid in school," Gershkowitz said. "And teasing him or taking advantage of him is a sure way to make a lot of enemies, including me."

"I can see he's a nice kid. I just meant, well, he's sort of simple, isn't he?"

"Just treat him right."

"Of course I will."

It was a long time later that I got to know the story behind Jeremy Holtz. What I learned about him first was that he was the best-liked individual at the Wheaton School. Everybody liked him—the preppies and the freaks and the misfits and the delinquents. There was never a party to which he was not invited and which he did not attend. He had gone to the Wheaton School since he was six. He was twenty-one when I met him.

He was the only son of the Holtz Petroleum family. His I.Q. was a two-digit number. He had his own psychiatrist—a famous one, whose only duty now was working with Jeremy—also a personal secretary and bodyguard, a Ph.D. psychologist who laid out his clothes, drove him to school, and, together with the psychiatrist, coached him in social skills. They had started with toilet training, which took a few years, moved on to the use of knife and fork, telling time, and making polite conversation. The end result was that he had the best manners of anybody in the school. Miss Josephine had him down for pre-med at Princeton.

August Holtz, his father, was a benefactor of the school. I also was told that Miss Roanoke, who taught Psychology and English, was regularly called in for consultations, but the significance of this was lost on me at the time.

XXXII

It was a few days before I found my way to the upper stories of the Wheaton School. I had attached myself to Clifton Fadiman, and went where he went. Clifton, besides putting in a great many hours at the Busy Bun, tended to operate in the basement of the school, the alley, the garage, the service entrance, the kitchen. He was on good terms with the help, all of whom were black and in whose company Clifton used black dialect. Sometimes we were joined by Jeremy Holtz, who was usually en route to help with some maintenance task.

The only times Clifton moved above ground level were at night, when he would sometimes visit Gershkowitz in his room. His other night haunts included various clubs and bars on the near North Side. He cultivated pimps, whores, and gamblers, and occasionally ran errands for them. He always wore cheap sharkskin suits, and wild neckties, striped shirts, and pointy black shoes. In season, he went to the racetrack regularly. Clifton appeared to live alone in a hotel room somewhere in the neighborhood. He had a father, who was always away.

Of course, I admired Clifton for serving an apprenticeship as a small-time underworld sleazeball while going to high school, but I was never invited to join in his nocturnal activity—and his accounts of the doings of the people he admired began to show a certain monotony.

"This guy Fritz—he's a horse player . . ."

"Yes?"

". . . and every night he has a fight with his girlfriend, who's a bimbo and hangs around the lobby of the Lincoln Park Hotel."

"So?"

"He comes in and accuses her of being a hooker, which of course she is."

"And?"

"Well, they holler at each other, and after a while the guy at the desk makes them leave."

"Then what happens?"

"They go across the street and have a hamburger at Mike's, and continue the fight."

"Um."

"It's funny. They do it every night."

Clifton had a style, but it needed something. He was beginning to bore me.

I knocked on Miss Jean's office door one day and asked if my program had been worked out. It hadn't. Miss Jean looked perturbed. She wrote out a schedule of classes on a card and handed it to me.

"Just go to these classes," she said. "I'll find out why you haven't been given the necessary placement tests, and after you've done them, we'll make any changes called for."

I had already gotten the measure of the place enough to know that there would never be any placement tests. I wandered up the staircase, looking for Miss Roanoke's English class.

I soon got to know my way around the Wheaton School. It put me in mind of places I had read about and seen in movies—Hole in the Wall, Dry Tortugas, outlaw settlements where bandits were welcome to take shelter. Here the dregs of Chicago youth turned up: delinquents, neurotics, idiots, freaks, and a few innocents whose parents were crazy enough to believe they were sending a child to a fancy private school in a fancy neighborhood.

Most of the kids, even the slow ones, knew what the place was and enjoyed interacting with the faculty (which was as unique as the student body—and in much the same way)—observing and adding to the chaos, and learning lessons few other schools have offered.

It was and is my opinion that it is a happy place. The

only sad note is struck by those few students who, with the Wheaton sisters, seem to buy into the fantasy that it is a genuine private school like Francis W. Parker, Bateman, and the Chicago Latin School—the inmates of which have nothing to do with us, on strict orders from their parents and teachers. Those kids—the prep-sters—work hard to sustain the appearance of well-bred and well-dressed children of good families, having a fine time in school and preparing for entrance to Eastern colleges.

The rest of us try to be kind to this lot. There are seven or eight of them altogether. In the Wheaton yearbook, except for the obligatory individual portraits of seniors, under each of which is a pack of lies includ-ing "College: Yale," or Harvard, Cornell, Princeton, etc., no kid is pictured more than once except that gang of smiling, cheerful, deluded pathetnoids. They are shown editing the nonexistent school paper, posing as the various nonexistent athletic teams, preparing dec-orations for dances which never took place—or ended as riots—meeting as student government, looking through a microscope, and sitting in class listening raptly to Mr. Fish, an entirely pointless exercise, since following his conversion to Babaism, he communicated exclusively by pointing to letters of the alphabet painted on a wooden paddle he carried with him.

On the positive side, people show respect and toler-ance at the Wheaton School. We are never warned against Jews or Communists. Mr. Baker is a proud card-carrying member of the Party, and I have to say is better than poor Sergeant Gunter at explaining dialectical materialism. There could hardly be any condemnation of homosexuals, given the presence of Mr. Saunders, big as three—and pornography is never mentioned, perhaps out of respect for Miss Roanoke.

XXXIII

Spring came, my first in Chicago, and at the Wheaton School. I can't say I didn't cut school, but I didn't cut more than a lot of people. The truth is, I cut a lot less than I had at Riverview. It was sort of accepted that students at Wheaton would wander off when they felt inclined, and wander back when they were ready.

Even though Wheaton was anarchic and chaotic, there was a minimum level of attendance called for. The wise student figured out just how often to show up and how much to participate in what passed for organized learning. "You never know," Miss Jean would say, "when the Board of Education might send an investigator." While it was tacitly understood that one's transcript would be all right, whatever happened, one still had to take the Scholastic Aptitude Tests, unless one was content to schlep off to the state university, which took everyone and then made freshman year as intolerable as possible so many would go away.

I never had a bad time or was actually bored when in the school. The teachers were all crazy in various endearing or interesting ways, and we kids did our best to contribute. You never knew when someone was going to have some kind of fit, say something hilariously inappropriate, or just look funny. Nastasia said it was like a mental hospital with (almost) nobody medicated and no doctors to spoil the fun. She was in a position to know.

Nastasia didn't make this remark directly to me, but in my presence. She had taken to never speaking to me at all. Instead, she stared at me with smoldering eyes and a fixed expression. This unnerved me. Frequently, when I thought I was alone, I would suddenly become aware of her, a little way off, giving me the stare. If I returned her gaze, or tried to speak to her, she would vanish, only to reappear in a few minutes, to stare some more.

Not that I had any aptitude for it, but I was unable to develop relationships with any of the girls at Wheaton. This was partly because I was scared of them, and partly because they were scared of her. It had crossed my mind that if I spent time with another girl, Nastasia might kill me, or do something equally unpleasant.

I was not without a social life at Wheaton. There were occasional parties, which ranged from boring failures to lively rumpuses with police called by the neighbors. I put in my time at the Busy Bun, smoking and joking with fellow students. I twice went to the opera, a guest of Jeremy Holtz, whose family had a box. I hung out a bit with Clifton Fadiman in the bowels of the school and visited Gershkowitz in his room. Sometimes Kenny Papescu appeared at school, and sometimes I would leave with him to help with a delivery.

When I was on my own, I continued to read in the public library, view movies at the Clark Theater, and attend lectures at the university.

In spring, with all the windows open, a kind of softness came over the Wheaton School. People went to classes in nearby Lincoln Park, or just went to the park. I found myself gazing at green buds for long periods, standing at the window of one of the bathrooms, savoring a cigar (I had moved up from Wolf Brothers Rum-Soaked Crooks to clear Havanas at twenty-five or even fifty cents apiece).

The bathrooms at Wheaton are a kind of neutral territory, where students and faculty can meet as equals and enjoy tobacco. As of my first spring, there were still a few gold faucets from the glory days of the house that Clifton Fadiman had not pried loose yet, and the tilework is of the best. They are more or less coed and function as lounges rather than lavatories. If one needs a bathroom for conventional purposes, there is a small one off the lobby.

I had gotten to love the house. Originally the mansion of Hamish MacTavish, a local robber baron, it was built at the turn of the century to be the finest house in the city.

We were slowly destroying it, but it was a real work of architecture. Even with all the costly furnishings replaced by desks and blackboards, we could still enjoy the graceful proportions of the rooms, the paneled walls, the ornate plaster ceilings, the staircase, and the library made of solid oak, with many of MacTavish's books still in place.

Sometimes Miss Jean plays the Steinway grand piano in the ballroom, with the tall windows and the chandelier, which we use for assemblies and sometimes as a gym. It's a nice place to listen to music.

A nice place to read, I discovered, is the roof, which has a balustrade with stone urns and odd carvings of bearded faces surrounded by leaves. Jeremy Holtz is the only other person who uses it. He reads there, too, mostly picture books from the lower-school library.

That spring I read *The Great Gatsby* and *Tender Is the Night* by F. Scott Fitzgerald, *Looking Backward* by Edward Bellamy, and the complete Fuzzy Bunny series, which I borrowed from Jeremy.

XXXIV

The school term didn't so much come to an end as trail off gradually. People came to school less and less as the weather got warmer, then hardly at all, and then not at all.

My final report card came in the mail. I had gotten A's and A+'s in everything, including German, a class I didn't know I was registered for and had certainly never attended.

Had I complained about this, I assume the office at Wheaton would have claimed it was a clerical mistake—but why complain? I was racking up useful credits and excellent grades. College was looking like a possibility. All the clerical errors were in the student's favor at Wheaton.

Along with the report card was a printed sheet, which my father read with interest.

"Looky dis, bum! It says here you can go to summer

school by those old ladies and get a whole year credits in t'ree months. Costs deh same as for a whole year almost, but you greduate next June, and I can kick your fet ass out from my house for good. I'm gonna sign you up, loafer. Det much sooner deh navy vill hev you."

My father had recently made a pile of money, in cash, out of a deal involving counterfeit hula hoops. Flush as he was, he had no reason to hesitate before paying the stiff fee for the Wheaton School Accelerated Summer School.

"Besides, you deserve it, mine boy. Look at deh excellent fake marks you got. Keep up deh good work."

I had nothing against the idea of summer school at Wheaton. I didn't expect it would make any unusual demands on my time, and it would prevent my father from insisting I find a real job.

I planned to work with Kenny as much as possible until he left for Paris with Linda, who had somehow passed all her courses at Riverview. Then I was going to work for Mr. Papescu, solo, and get Kenny's pay until he came back, which he was claiming would be never. Mr. Papescu had bribed some inspector, and I had a driver's license. Before he left, Kenny was going to teach me how to actually drive.

I once commented to Kenny that I could, theoretically, pass courses by doing work, and get a driver's license by learning how to drive first and then taking the test. Kenny said it was his opinion I thought that way because I wasn't brought up in Chicago. He said that doing things the regular way was uncreative and might become a habit in later life. He said it was a good thing I had met him, found out about the Wheaton School, and had begun to develop my creativity. I have to say, I agree with him.

Summer in Chicago is a sweaty, humid, smelly heaven. Everything slows down. People who have been walking fast with their heads down during the bitter winter begin to stroll, looking around at things, swinging their arms. When the breeze is right, you can hear the cheering from Wrigley Field, where the Cubs play. The stands are full at afternoon games on week-days—people taking creative leave from their jobs. When the breeze is wrong, you can smell the stock-yards from all the way south.

At night, people sit outside while they wait for their apartments to cool down. Some people sleep in the park, next to the lake. It's as though everyone has moved their living rooms into the street. Sometimes you'll see people who have set up a card table and chairs under a streetlight having a game of gin rummy.

I learned about sidewalk standing. It goes like this: After supper one wanders out of one's apartment building. Right there, or within a couple of blocks, there will be a little group of teenagers standing on the sidewalk, leaning against buildings or against cars.

Everybody is smoking. The girls tend to clump together, and the boys holler and show off for the girls. People talk and watch the fireflies.

At a certain point the little group will start moving in the direction of Lake Shore Drive. There's no decision to move—it just happens. Along the way, the group may meet other groups, with which it mingles, and those groups begin to move, too.

When the groups reach Lake Shore Drive, they will have increased to bands numbering twenty or thirty. These bands will drift southward, encountering other bands, until a pack forms amounting to maybe a hundred, stretched out a block's length, heading south.

At Oak Street, two or three packs will converge, and a herd of adolescents will cross Lake Shore Drive and join the huge mass of kids on the lakefront. Cigarettes are smoked, beer is consumed, there is running and jumping behavior, some threats, rarely a fight, flirting and necking, yelling and joking, until the cops show up around midnight and chase us off the beach.

I know this sounds mindless, and I thought so, too, but I did it night after night.

XXXV

I improved my nocturnal activities by emulating Wally Gershkowitz, who was one of the two teachers in the Wheaton Accelerated Summer School. The other was Mr. Baker.

Gershkowitz spent most of his evenings at the famous College of Complexes, one of the few bars in Chicago where a minor could not get a drink. I believe the management was conscientious about this, not because of scruples, but because teenagers, such as myself, would have lowered the tone of the scheduled entertainment, which included goofy panel discussions and lectures, elaborate word games, poetry, and jazz. I once had a peek inside—everything was bathed in a strange gray-blue light that gave a dreamlike quality to the scene. Little signs painted on cardboard hung on strings from the ceiling. I couldn't make out what was printed on them, but I was sure it was witty as all get-out. I would have died to get into that place.

However, I was welcome at Gershkowitz's other haunt, Maxie's Bookshop, right across the street from Bughouse Square, the free-speech park and outdoor mental ward. This is a bookstore, closed all day and open all night, which has never sold a book, although they do have some, and browsers and borrowers are encouraged. The place is crowded with loonies, lonelys, speakers, listeners, debaters, radicals, beatniks, artists, insomniacs, and chess players. There is a long table at the back of the store with chess boards and a number of games going on, and being kibitzed, at all times.

William Lloyd Floyd, whose business card reads "Manager and Resident Philosopher," has a huge beard, a bald head, and wears a large Byzantine cross on his turtleneck. He organizes debates and discussions among the regulars. As I understand it, Maxie's is regarded by those who frequent it as a more serious place than the College of Complexes, though it is also said that the crowd at Maxie's is less intelligent, and too poor or cheap, to spring for the price of a drink.

Black coffee is available at Maxie's, and around midnight, the old hunchbacked guy goes out for a loaf of white bread and a hunk of blue cheese. You can toss some coins into a can toward costs, or not. The crowd is mostly male, but there are a few women regulars, dressed all in black, with pale white makeup, applied the standard beatnik way, covering face, lips, and eyebrows. On weekends, tourists drift in, and the nightly types pounce on them as a fresh audience for their favorite routines.

I enjoy the Rhinoceros Milk Man. This is not a brand-name health-food product—you have to make it yourself—and the Rhinoceros Milk Man, in addition to making elaborate claims for the benefits, repeats the formula, including brewer's yeast, black-strap molasses, bone meal, and God knows what else. His big finish is to whip off his hat and point to a few lonely strands. "See that? I used to be bald as a post!"

There is an Indian, who always wears a suit, and taught me a few useful tricks of basic Yoga. And a professional chess player who looks like Bela Lugosi and always wears his jacket buttoned up to the neck. When he is in a tight spot in a game, he'll undo his jacket to reveal a hand-painted necktie so lurid that his opponent loses concentration.

William Lloyd Floyd, for a considerable period of time, had set up to write a book. He had an ancient Underwood, on one side of which was a thick stack of typing paper, and on the other side of which was a pile of finished manuscript, as high as the typewriter itself. He would sit, typing steadily through all the hollering and tumult, joining in the conversation himself, whipping out finished pages, and rolling in fresh paper at a brisk rate. Anyone could have a look at what he was typing. It appeared to be gibberish.

Sometimes a painter will drag in a bunch of canvases and improvise an exhibition. The regulars do not withhold comments and criticism, insults and encouragement. The place is always lively. In fact, I can only remember one time when a pall fell over the proceedings—a bunch of genuine, New York City beatniks, on their way to Mexico, dropped in. They scared us. They were mean, sullen, and taciturn, manifestly unwashed, and had the expression of beasts. Most of the Maxie's crowd had day jobs, though they avoided admitting it. Except for a character named Fallout, our pet junkie, almost nobody used. And none of us had body lice or scales on the soles of our feet. Confronted by the real thing, we had to admit to ourselves that we were soft, good-natured, Midwestern bozos compared to actual beatniks.

Gershkowitz himself came from New York. He fell somewhere to the left of the Chicago beats, or quasi-beats, but was not quite as fierce as those Eastern types who had shaken us up. It was easy to imagine him, in an earlier incarnation, tossing bombs at the Czar. He had that look.

XXXVI

I hadn't had Gershkowitz for a class during the term. He and Mr. Baker were supposed to get the summer-school students, numbering five in all, through a year's worth of learning in a single summer.

"This is easier than it sounds," Gershkowitz said. "Since Wheaton students learn approximately nothing during the average year, duplicating that, or even improving on it, is hardly a challenge. However, to amuse myself, I intend to actually teach you a year's worth, in quality if not quantity.

"Here is the first lesson. I have in mind a certain number. I will not tell you what it is, but the student who is absent for that number of days in a row will receive a failing grade for the whole summer school— and as always at Wheaton, there are no refunds."

There was silence as the four students present calculated. It was unlikely that Gershkowitz would flunk us for being absent for a day—or he'd have to flunk every-body. Two days was unlikely as well, though not out of the question, but three . . . three might be possible.

Roger Silver raised his hand. "Mr. Gershkowitz, are we expected to be here for the entire day?"

"That would be too inhumane, even for me," Gersh-kowitz said.

It was obvious. To eliminate the possibility of falling afoul of Gershkowitz's rule, all one had to do was show his face every day, after which one could do as one pleased.

"The other thing which will have you explaining to your parents why you got no credit for their consider-able investment is this: On those occasions when I do see you, you must have a book in your immediate pos-session, and be prepared to talk to me about it, should I ask you. I don't care what book it is, but have a care—I am easily bored. If you show up with the same book more than three times in a row—twice if it's a boring book—I will fail you."

Gershkowitz smiled frighteningly. "Oh yes, you'd better remember this, too. I get cruel when I am bored. It would be a mistake to bore me."

This was, so far, the most fun I had ever had in a classroom.

It got better. Mr. Baker taught in a fairly normal way, by lecturing, assigning reading and papers, and giving tests. He got the usual Wheaton School response, maybe a little better, as there were only five of us in the summer school and it was relatively difficult to hide. Mr. Baker was an interesting teacher, especially when he got excited and his dentures flew out.

Gershkowitz employed what he called an intellectual scavenger hunt, or challenge questions. He would bark out topics to all of us, or one topic to a student. Then we were expected to scurry off and find out as much as we could about the topic he had barked.

For example, he might say, "Nifkin! The legend of Theseus! Thursday!"

This meant I had until Thursday to find out all I could about the legend of Theseus, and to prepare myself to answer whatever questions Gershkowitz might ask. He might say, "Nifkin! Tell me everything about Theseus," or he might ask, "Did you find out all about the Minotaur?" and then ask no more questions about the topic.

Sometimes you could look up the answers in encyclopedias, and sometimes you had to actually go around the city to find them. For example, Gershkowitz once bellowed, "Nifkin! What does *Ars longa, vita brevis* mean? Hint: It's over the inner doorway of a building downtown. Abraham Lincoln spoke there, and John Wilkes Booth acted there. What's the building?"

I found out that *Ars longa, vita brevis* means "Art lasts long, life is short," in Latin, and took the bus to the

Fine Arts building on Michigan Avenue. Sure enough, there it was in bronze letters over the archway of the inner door. There's an old theater on the first floor, and it was easy to guess that both Lincoln and his assassin, Booth, had each appeared there at some point. It's a neat old building, and I wandered around observing the architecture and decor. Pleased with myself, I put together a few notes about Chicago architecture I had picked up whiling away time at lectures at the University of Chicago, and held forth for about twenty minutes the next day at school.

"Not bad, Nifkin," Gershkowitz said. "But for some reason, you never mentioned the Monadnock Building. Tell me all about it tomorrow."

The Monadnock Building, sixteen stories, located at 53 West Jackson, was built in 1891 by John Root. It's the world's tallest building bearing its own weight. The walls are six feet thick at the bottom. I threw in some remarks about the Pontiac Building across the street, built the same year; it's an early example of a steel-frame skyscraper.

Sometimes we'd team up on an answer. When Gershkowitz said he would give a silver dollar to the person who brought six *char-shu-bao* to class the next day, Jack Evergreen and I hit Chinatown at Cermak Road and Wentworth Avenue. We had some trouble finding *char-shu-bao*, because they call them *da-ssu-ma* here. The guy in the greasy chopstick said that *char-*

shu-bao is what they call them in New York, which is where Gershkowitz comes from. They're steamed buns with a little piece of pork or a hunk of lotus root in the middle. Not bad, and pretty filling at fifteen cents apiece. Gershkowitz's silver dollar turned out to be a refund for the cost of the things.

Mr. Baker told us about *The Autobiography of Benvenuto Cellini* and made it sound so interesting that we all read it.

XXXVII

Here are some other books I read all or part of during the summer:

Twelve Against the Gods by William Bolitho. One of my favorites of the summer. Biographies of historical types who did big things.

The Adventures of Hajji Baba of Ispahan by James Morier. This is a picaresque novel, "picaresque" being one of Gershkowitz's words of the day. A cool book.

A Portrait of the Artist as a Young Man by James Joyce. A novel about a kid in Ireland.

Twenty Years at Hull-House by Jane Addams. The lady who invented the settlement house, which is still there, and I have been there.

Christ in Concrete by Pietro Di Donato. This is a great blood-and-guts novel.

The Saga of Gretti the Strong. I finally read one of those Icelandic things, or tried to.

The Theory of the Leisure Class by Thorstein Veblen. This guy explains everything about the society in which we live.

Confessions of an English Opium Eater by Thomas De Quincey. A little long. I didn't finish it. It's about a literary type in London.

The Adventures of Sherlock Holmes by Sir Arthur Conan Doyle. Far better than the TV show.

Rootabaga Stories by Carl Sandburg. Cool kids' stories. I don't know why I like them, but I do.

Up From Slavery by Booker T. Washington. He did it all, saw it all, tells his story.

The Perfumed Garden by Sheikh Nefzawi, translated by Richard Burton. How to do sex. I need a clearer book.

XXXVIII

Gershkowitz and Mr. Baker took us on field trips. In addition to the Art Institute almost every week (favorite paintings: *Nighthawks* by Edward Hopper, *Sunday Afternoon on the Island of La Grand Jatte* by Georges Seurat, and *Excavation* by Willem de Kooning), they took us to the Gate of Horn, a folk club, where we heard Odetta, this gorgeous big woman with the most amazing voice in the world. It turned out Gershkowitz knew her slightly, and she sat at our table for five minutes. None of us kids had the nerve to say a word in her presence.

They also took us to some blues clubs, and allowed us to drink beer. Mr. Baker, in his greasy double-breasted suit, with the rimless glasses and loose dentures, was a strange sight to us in settings like that, but he had the best time of anybody and drank a lot.

"Half the population and more than half the culture

in this city is black," Gershkowitz said. "You can't call yourself educated if you don't know anything about it."

Other assignments included catching certain films at the Clark Theater. We saw and discussed *Citizen Kane, Nosferatu* and *The Cabinet of Dr. Caligari* on a double bill, *Metropolis, Les Enfants du Paradis,* and *I Walked with a Zombie.*

Poetry and civics were covered by attending reading and debate nights at Maxie's bookstore and ordinary evenings at Bughouse Square across the street. Each of us was required to stand before an audience of strangers and read a poem we had written. We all went for haiku, because they're short. Here's mine:

> wind blows off lake
> freezing my butt
> stop for hot dog
> hot grease
> burns my lips

It went over fairly well, and I wrote a few more for my own amusement.

I was delighted to be reuinted with my old R.O.T.C. sergeant, citizen Gunter, who was preaching the gospel according to Karl Marx at Bughouse Square one night. He was glad to see me and had a lively conversation with Gershkowitz. It turned out that Gunter had been an intelligence officer during World War II, worked in the War Room at Allied Headquarters, and saw Eisenhower every day.

Gershkowitz wanted to know what our President had been like in those days.

"About the same as now," Gunter said. "Nice guy, in his way. I used to warn him about the military industrial complex after the war. He personally took care of my recent little rap with the F.B.I."

"Wow, the President got you off?" I was impressed.

"Even though we differ politically," Gunter said. "Old soldiers stick together."

To cover the science part of our summer curriculum, Gershkowitz talked to us about quantum physics, coached those interested (not me) in math, and took us on a field trip to the city morgue.

Then there was Gershkowitz's word of the day. Every day he'd give us a word, and we were supposed to find out what it meant and add it to our soon-to-be-mighty vocabularies.

Obambulate v. To wander or walk about in an aimless fashion.

Nyctophoniac a. Able to give voice only at night.

Invultuation n. The practice of sticking pins into a doll to cause pain to a person represented by the doll.

Flabellation n. The use of a fan to cool something.

Proctalgia n. A pain in the ass.

And, finest of the whole summer: *Gynotikolobomas-*

sophile n. one who likes to nibble the earlobes of women.

Jack Evergreen and I became fascinated by the chess games at Maxie's one night. We decided to learn the game. We asked Gershkowitz to teach us.

He agreed, but first he had something to say: "I must tell you, gentlemen, that the one thing I regret, more than any other thing, is having learned to play chess in my youth. Also, that I have no respect for anyone who is not a fairly decent chess player. Third, I take chess seriously—and anyone who doesn't ought not to play. Think it over, and if you still want me to teach you, come back in a week."

We came back. We showed Gershkowitz the beginner's chess books we had bought, and he gave us a lesson that consumed all the mental capacity we had. One more tiny fragment of information would not have fit. Our heads had never been so full. "Now go away and play a hundred games," Gershkowitz said. "Then come back for your next lesson."

Jack Evergreen and I began playing on the portable sets we had bought in the dime store and now carried at all times. We played in the library at school. We played in the park. We played under streetlights. We played on buses.

When we weren't playing, we studied our chess books. We talked about the Ruy López opening and the Petroff defense. We hung over the shoulders of old guys playing chess at Bughouse Square, and the chess hustlers and addicts at Maxie's.

After about a week, when I closed my eyes, I'd see chess diagrams—those little square chessboards, fuzzily printed like in the chess book, with the symbols of the pieces in various arrangements.

Jack and I had more or less stopped speaking English and expressed ourselves in chess terms: pawn to king 4; pawn to king's bishop 4; knight to king's bishop 3, and so forth. We already knew the names of the world's top chess players, and rooted for some, hated others, and argued with each other about which ones were the greatest.

We stopped doing any of the summer-school work. The books we carried with us, on pain of receiving no credit for the whole summer, were chess books. We tried to get Gershkowitz to talk about chess all the time—but he refused and quoted Fallout, the lovable junkie who hung out at Maxie's: "Each man chooses the drug he uses."

One night, during the second week of chess-madness, I woke up scared. I found out what a cold sweat was. If it had not been for Jack Evergreen, I might not have realized what danger I was in until much later—too late. Jack had already given his life to chess. He would not go to college, never take a job that would interfere with thinking about chess, not associate with, or be able to talk to, people who weren't involved in chess—live a mostly solitary life, inside his head—and all to worship the beauty of a game of which most people in this country don't even know the rules.

I decided to cop out. I was going to leave Jack to his fate. On the one hand, I envied him for loving something that much. I wanted to think that I was willing to make a sacrifice that big—but I knew I didn't want to make it for the game of chess. I tried to explain this to Jack, who looked at me as though I didn't know what I was talking about, and went back to his chess book.

XXXIX

Summer went by awfully fast, it seemed to me. Our last field trip was to the Bohemian Beer Garden. Wally Gershkowitz, Mr. Baker, and the five students in the Wheaton School Accelerated Summer School—Jack, Roger Silver, Richard Mamzer, Nicholas Podgorny, and myself—had a celebration. We ate salami sandwiches on pumpernickel and drank beer. Mr. Baker taught us a song in Latin, *"Gaudeamus Igitur,"* and we sang it over and over, with arms linked, rocking from side to side.

At the end of the celebration, Gershkowitz gave us each a certificate. At the top was printed: "The Wheaton School" in Old English lettering. Beneath was a printer's cut of an American eagle, with a banner in its beak bearing the words "State Sovereignty, National Union." Under that it said: "This is to certify that *Robert*

Nifkin has completed a full year of high school study in a single summer." Then there was a quotation in Latin: *Fiat Experimentum in Corpore Vili.*

It was signed at the bottom by Mr. Baker and Gershkowitz.

XL

"It is time to talk about the future," Gershkowitz said. "Since the Wheaton School's policy is to fake transcripts, and since it is somehow accredited, through what kind of crooked fix-up I cannot say, students from here, in theory, can be admitted to colleges. The failsafe, for the colleges, is the personal interview. Those of your fellow pupils who drool and can't make complete sentences or tie their own shoes are likely to be spotted at this point and won't get in.

"You, Nifkin, while slightly repellant, do not actually present yourself as a borderline case, so it is possible that some college will actually take you. Is this your desire?"

I told him it was.

"Did you have a college in mind?"

I didn't.

"I have one in mind for you. It's St. Leon's."

"Why there?" I asked him.

"It's progressive. They give a lot of freedom to the students. It's got a pretty campus, and you're just about certain to get laid."

"I want to go there," I said.

XLI

I was actually ebullient, elated, euphoric, and exhilarated when the fall semester at Wheaton began. I was glad to see the moronic faces of the morons, the twitchy faces of the neurotics, the evil faces of the criminals, the frustrated, bewildered faces of the faculty, and the sweet smiling faces of Miss Jean and Miss Josephine.

There were new students, who had been purged out of the official education system. Each of them would make his or her contribution to the life of our little school. Janice Steinway, a tall blond freshman, attracted a lot of attention, as she appeared to be especially willing to contribute.

The former members of the Accelerated Summer School were energized when the fall semester began. We would leave beloved old Wheaton School in the spring, and we were determined to learn all we could while we had the opportunity. Baker and Gershkowitz had gotten us addicted.

All but Jack Evergreen, who did not return to school at the end of the summer. He's in San Francisco, working in a bakery called the Dharma Bun. He sent me a couple of postcards with seventeen-syllable poems about playing chess with Lawrence Ferlinghetti.

All the students were sad to learn of Miss Roanoke's arrest. We hoped her lawyer would get her off, but we knew, even if she was acquitted, she couldn't be a teacher again—even at Wheaton. This was an example of bourgeois hypocrisy. I am certain she never corrupted my morals.

Nastasia, the bereaved daughter of Miles Greenthorpe, has continued her policy of not speaking to me, but initiated the practice of dragging me into closets and French-kissing me. This unnerved me the first couple of times, but I soon learned to look forward to it. I am hoping our relationship will continue to develop, including longer periods of physical contact in less confined spaces.

Jeremy Holtz is already accepted at Princeton.

Linda and Kenny came back from Paris. They say they missed cheeseburgers. They're going to get married when Linda graduates. Kenny's taking night classes in Psych. at Amundson Junior College. He says he wants to be a psychotherapist. Dr. Pudovkin is paying his tuition.

Sergeant Gunter is happy. He's one of the most popular speakers at Bughouse Square, and while he doesn't entirely approve of the beatniks at Maxie's, they all like him, and he hangs out there almost every night.

My parents are happy. They are going to gold-leaf the walls of the living room.

And I am happy—or I will be when I know for sure that I am going to be allowed to continue my education in a fine and venerable institution like St. Leon's College.

This essay is respectfully submitted by:
Robert Nifkin, Chicago, October 1958